the store of a million items

fiction by MICHELLE CLIFF

NO TELEPHONE TO HEAVEN

BODIES OF WATER (*stories*)

FREE ENTERPRISE

ABENG

the store of a million items

STORIES

Michelle Cliff

A Mariner Original

HOUGHTON MIFFLIN COMPANY

BOSTON · NEW YORK 1998

For information about permission to reproduce
selections from this book, write to Permissions,
Houghton Mifflin Company, 215 Park Avenue
South, New York, New York 10003.

Library of Congress Cataloging-in-Publication Data
Cliff, Michelle.
    The store of a million items : stories / Michelle Cliff.
        p. cm.
    "A Mariner original."
    Contents: Transactions — Monsters — Contagious
melancholia — Down the shore — The store of a million
items — Stan's speed shop — Wartime — Art history
— Rubicon — Apache tears — A public woman.
    ISBN 0-395-90129-4
    I. Title.
    PR9265.9.C55S86   1998
    813 — dc21   97-43805 CIP

Printed in the United States of America

Book design by Robert Overholtzer

QUM 10 9 8 7 6 5 4 3 2 1

Some of these stories originally appeared in the follow-
ing publications: *Tri-Quarterly; Best American Short
Stories 1997; American Voice; Women: A Cultural Review;
Voice Literary Supplement; Agni; Southwest Review.*

You will be saved from the strange woman,
from the foreign woman with her smooth words.

— PROVERBS 2:16

contents

one

TRANSACTIONS ✦ 3

MONSTER ✦ 20

CONTAGIOUS MELANCHOLIA ✦ 30

two

DOWN THE SHORE ✦ 39

THE STORE OF A MILLION ITEMS ✦ 42

STAN'S SPEED SHOP ✦ 55

WARTIME ✦ 64

ART HISTORY ✦ 75

three

RUBICON ✦ 93

APACHE TEARS ✦ 102

A PUBLIC WOMAN ✦ 109

part one

transactions

I

A BLOND, BLUE-EYED CHILD, about three years old — no one will know her exact age, ever — is sitting in the clay of a country road, as if she and the clay are one, as if she is the first human, but she is not.

She is dressed in a boy's shirt, sewn from osnaburg check, which serves her as a dress. Her face is scabbed. The West Indian sun, even at her young age, has made rivulets underneath her eyes where waters run.

She is always hungry.

She works the clay into a vessel which will hold nothing.

Lizards fly between the tree ferns that stand at the roadside.

A man is driving an American Ford, which is black and eating up the sun. He wears a Panama hat with a red band around it. He carries a different brightly colored band for each day of the week. He is pale and the band interrupts his paleness. His head is balding and he takes care to conceal his naked crown. In his business, appearance is important.

He is practicing his Chinese as he negotiates the mountain road, almost washed away by the rains of the night before. His abacus rattles on the seat beside him. With each swerve and bump, and there are many, the beads of the abacus quiver and slide.

He is alone.

"You should see some of these shopkeepers, my dear," he tells his wife, "they make this thing sing."

His car is American and he has an American occupation. He is a traveling salesman. He travels into the interior of the island, his car packed with American goods.

Many of the shopkeepers are Chinese, but like him, like everyone it seems, are in love with American things. He brings American things into the interior, into the clearing cut from ruinate. Novelties and necessities. Witch hazel. Superman. Band-Aids. Zane Grey. Chili con carne. Cap guns. Coke syrup. Fruit cocktail. Camels.

Marmalade and Marmite, Bovril and Senior Service, the weekly *Mirror* make room on the shopkeepers' shelves.

The salesman has always wanted a child. His wife says she never has. "Too many pickney in the world already," she says, then kisses her teeth. His wife is brown-skinned. He is not. He is pale, with pale eyes.

The little girl sitting in the road could be his, but the

environment of his wife's vagina is acid. And then there is her brownness. Well.

And then he sees her. Sitting filthy and scabbed in the dirt road as he comes around a corner counting to a hundred in Chinese. She is crying.

Has he startled her?

He stops the car.

He and his wife have been married for twenty years. They no longer sleep next to each other. They sleep American-style as his wife calls it. She has noticed that married couples in the movies sleep apart. In "Hollywood" beds. She prevails on Mr. Dickens (a handyman she is considering bringing into the house in broad daylight) to construct "Hollywood" beds from mahogany.

The salesman gets out of the car and walks over to the little girl.

He asks after her people.

She points into the bush.

He lifts her up. He uses his linen hanky to wipe off her face. He blots her eye-corners, under her nose. He touches her under her chin.

"Lord, what a solemn lickle ting."

He hears her tummy grumble.

At the edge of the road there is a narrow path down a steep hillside.

The fronds of a coconut tree cast shadows across the scabs on her face. He notices they are rusty. They will need attention.

He thinks he has a plan.

At the end of the narrow path is a clearing with some mauger dogs, packed red-dirt yard, and a wattle house set on cement blocks.

The doorway, there is no door, yawns into the darkness.

He walks around the back, still holding the child, the dogs sniffing at him, licking at the little girl's bare feet.

A woman, blond and blue-eyed, is squatting under a tree. He is afraid to approach any closer, afraid she is engaged in some intimate activity, but soon enough she gets up, wipes her hand on her dress, and walks toward him.

Yes, this is her little girl, the woman says in a strangely accented voice. And the salesman realizes he's stumbled on the descendants of a shipload of Germans, sent here as convicts or cheap labor, he can't recall which. There are to this day pockets of them in the deep bush.

He balances the little girl in one arm — she weighs next to nothing — removes his hat, inclines his balding head toward the blonder woman. She lowers her blue eyes. One eye has a cloud, the start of a cataract from too much sun.

He knows what he wants.

The woman has other children, sure, too many, she says. He offers twenty American dollars, just like that, counting out the single notes, and promises the little girl will have the best of everything, always, and that he loves children and has always wanted one of his own but he and his wife have never been so blessed.

The woman says something he does not understand. She points to a small structure at the side of the house. Under a peaked roof is a statue of the Virgin Mary, a dish of water at her feet. On her head is a coronet of *lignum vitae*. She is rude but painted brightly, like the Virgins at the roadside in Bavaria, carved along routes of trade and plague. Her shawl is colored indigo.

"Liebfrau," the woman repeats.

He nods.

The Virgin's shawl is flecked with yellow, against indigo, like the Milky Way against the black of space.

The salesman is not Catholic but never mind. He promises the little girl will attend the Convent of the Immaculate Conception at Constant Spring, the very best girls' school on the island. He goes on about their uniforms. Very handsome indeed. Royal blue neckties and white dresses. Panama hats with royal blue hatbands. He points to the band around his own hat by way of explanation.

The royal blue will make his daughter's eyes bright.

This woman could not be more of a wonder to him. She is a stranger in this landscape, this century, she of an indentured status, a petty theft.

He wonders at her loneliness. No company but the Virgin Mother.

The woman extends her hand for the money, puts it in the side pocket of her dress. She strokes the head of her daughter, still in the salesman's arms.

"She can talk?"

"Jah, no mus'?"

A squall comes from inside the darkness of the house, and the woman turns, her dress becoming damp.

"Well, goodbye then," the salesman says.

She turns back. She opens her dress and presses a nipple, dripping, into the mouth of her little girl. "Bye, bye," she says. And she is gone.

He does not know what to think.

The little girl makes no fuss, not even a whimper, as he carries her away, and he is suddenly afraid he has purchased damaged goods. What if she's foolish? It will be difficult enough to convince his brown-skinned wife to bring a white-skinned child into the house. If she is fool-fool God help him.

Back at the car he tucks her into the front seat, takes his penknife and opens a small tin of fruit cocktail.

He points to the picture on the label, the glamorous maraschino cherry. "Wait till you taste this, darlin'. It come all the way from America." Does she have the least sense of what America is?

He wipes away the milk at the corners of her mouth.

He takes a spoon from the glove compartment.

"You can feed yourself?"

She says nothing, so he begins to spoon the fruit cocktail into her. Immediately she brightens and opens her mouth wide, tilting her head back like a little bird.

In no time she's finished the tin.

"Mustn't eat too fast, sweetheart. Don't want to get carsick."

"Nein, nein," she says with a voice that's almost a growl.

She closes her eyes against the sun flooding the car.

"Never mind," he says, "we'll be off soon." He wraps the spoon and empty fruit cocktail tin into a sheet of the *Daily Gleaner*, putting the package on the floor of the back seat.

Next time he will pour some condensed milk into the tinned fruit, making it even sweeter.

There's a big American woman who runs a restaurant outside Milk River. She caters to the tourists who come to take the famously radioactive waters. And to look at the crocodiles. She also lets rooms. She will let him a room for the night. In return he will give her the American news she craves. She says she once worked in the movies. He doesn't know if he believes her.

He puts the car in gear and drives away from the clearing.

His heart is full. Is this how women feel? he wonders, as he glances at the little girl, now fast asleep.

What has he done? She is his treasure, his newfound thing, and he never even asked her name. What will you call this child? the priest will ask. Now she is yours. He must have her baptized. Catholic or Anglican, he will decide.

He will have to bathe her. He will ask the American woman to help him. He will take a bathroom at the mineral spring and dip her into the famous waters, into the "healing stream," like the old song says.

He will baptize her himself. The activity of the spring, of world renown, will mend her skin. The scabs on her face are crusted over and there are more on her arms and legs. She might well have scurvy, even in the midst of a citrus grove.

But the waters are famous.

As he drives he alternates between making plans and

imagining his homecoming and his wife's greeting. You must have taken leave of your senses, busha. She calls him busha when she's angry and wants him to stand back. No, busha. Is who tell you we have room fi pickney? He will say he had no choice. Was he to leave this little girl in the middle of a country road covered with dirt and sores and hungry? Tell me, busha, tell me jus' one ting: Is how many pickney you see this way on your travels, eh? Is why you don't bring one home sooner? Tell me that.

Everybody wants a child that favors them, that's all.

She will kiss her teeth.

If she will let him have his adoption, he will say, she can have the other side of the house for her and Mr. Dickens. It will be simple. Once he plays that card there will be no going back. They will split the house down the middle. That will be that.

Like is drawn to like. Fine to fine. Coarse to coarse.

There are great advantages to being a traveling salesman in this place. He learns the island by heart. Highland and floodplain, sinkhole and plateau. Anywhere a shopkeeper might toss up, fix some shelves inside a zinc-roofed shed, open shop.

He respects the relentlessness of shopkeepers. They will nest anywhere. You can be in the deepest bush and come upon a tin sign advertising Nescafé, and find a group of people gathered as if the shed were a town hall, which it well might be.

Everything is commerce, he cannot live without it.

On the road sometimes he is taken by what is around him. He is distracted by gorges, ravines possessed of an uncanny green. Anything could dwell there. If he looks closer, he will enter the island's memory, the petroglyphs of a disappeared people. The birdmen left by the Arawak.

Once he took a picnic lunch of cassava cake and fried fish and ginger beer into the burial cave at White Marl and left a piece of cassava at the feet of one of the skeletons.

He gazes at the remains of things. Stone fences, fallen, moss-covered, which might mark a boundary in Somerset. Ruined windmills. A circular ditch where a coffle marked time on a treadmill. As steady as an orbit.

A salesman is free, he tells himself. He makes his own hours, comes and goes as he pleases. People look forward to his arrival, and not just for the goods he carries. He is part troubador. If he's been to the movies in town he will recount the plot for a crowd, describe the beauty of the stars, the screen washed in color.

These people temper his loneliness.

But now, now.

Now he thinks he'll never be lonely again.

II

The Bath is located on the west bank of Milk River, just south of where the Rio Brontë, much tamer than its name, branches off.

The waters of the Bath rise through the karst, the heart of stone. The ultimate source of the Bath is an underground saline spring, which might suggest a relationship with the sea. The relationship with the sea is suggested everywhere; the limestone that composes more of the land than any other substance is nothing but the skeletons of marine creatures.

"From the sea we come, to the sea we shall return." His nursemaid used to chant this as he lay in his pram on King's Parade.

The water of the Bath is a steady temperature of ninety-one degrees Fahrenheit (thirty-three degrees Centigrade). The energy of the water is radiant, fifty-five times more active than Baden-Baden, fifty times more active than Vichy.

Such is the activity that bathers are advised not to remain immersed for more than fifteen minutes a day.

In the main building the bather may read testimonials to the healing faculties of the waters. These date to 1794, when the first bathrooms were opened.

> Lord Salisbury was cured of lowness of spirit
> Hamlet, his slave, escaped depraved apprehensions
> MAY 1797, ANNO DOMINI

> Mrs. Horne was cured of the hysteria and loss of spleen
> DECEMBER 1802, ANNO DOMINI

> The Governor's Lady regained her appetites
> OCTOBER 1817, ANNO DOMINI

> Septimus Hart, Esq., banished his dread
> JULY 1835, ANNO DOMINI

The Hon. Catherine Dillon was cured of a mystery
FEBRUARY 1900, ANNO DOMINI

The waters bore magical properties. Indeed, some thought the power of the Lord was in them.

The salesman's car glides into the gravel parking lot of the Little Hut, the American woman's restaurant. She named it after a movie she made with Ava Gardner and Stewart Granger. A movie she made sounds grandiose; she picked up after Miss Gardner, stood in for her during long shots.

She hears the car way back in the kitchen of the restaurant, where she's supervising Hamlet VII in the preparation of dinner. Tonight, pepper pot soup to start, followed by curried turtle, rice and peas, a Bombay mango cut in half and filled with vanilla ice cream.

The American woman, her head crowned with a thick black braid, comes out of the doorway onto the verandah that runs around the Little Hut and walks toward the salesman's car.

"Well, well, what have we got here?" She points to the passenger seat in front. "What are you? A kidnapper or something?"

She's wearing a khaki shirt with red and black epaulets, the tails knotted at her midsection, and khaki shorts. The kitchen steam has made her clothes limp, and sweat stains bloom on her back and under her arms. Her feet are bare. She wears a silver bangle around one ankle.

"Gone native" is one of her favorite ways of describing

herself, whether it means bare feet, a remnant of chain, or swimming in Milk River alongside the crocodiles.

Still she depends on the salesman to bring her news of home.

"I've got your magazines, your *Jets*," the salesman says, ignoring her somewhat bumptious remark.

It was late afternoon by now. A quick negotiation about a room for the night and then he will take his little sleepyhead, who has not stirred, to be bathed. He has great faith in the waters from all he has heard.

He asks the American woman about a room.

"There's only one available right now," she tells him. "I've been overrun."

The room is located behind the restaurant, next to the room where Hamlet VII sleeps.

The salesman, she remembers his name is Harold (he was called "Prince Hal" at school he told her), hers is Rosalind, is not crazy about sleeping in what he considers servants' quarters and tells her so.

"My daughter," he begins.

Rosalind interrupts him. "You may as well take it."

He's silent.

"It's clean and spacious," she tells him, "lots of room for you, and for her." She nods in the direction of the little girl. She can't help but be curious, aware from his earlier visits that he said he had no children, that his wife had turned her back on him, or so he said, that he equated being a traveler for an import firm with being a pirate on the Spanish Main, right down to the ribbon on his hat and his galleon of a car.

"Footloose and fancy-free" was how he described himself to her, but Rosalind didn't buy it.

He seemed like a remnant to her. So many of them did. There was something behind the thickness of green, in the crevices of bone; she wore a sign of it on her ankle.

"Very well, then. I'll take it."

"You won't be sorry."

"I need to take her to the Bath presently. Will you come?"

"Me? Why?"

"I need a woman to help me with her."

"I thought you said she was your daughter."

"I did."

"What's wrong with her?"

"Her skin is broken."

"Well, they have attendants at the Bath to help you."

"Okay, then."

Rosalind had in mind a stack of *Jets*, a pitcher of iced tea, and a break into the real world, Chicago, New York, Los Angeles, before the deluge of bathers, thirsty for something besides radioactive waters, descended on her.

"It will be fine. Just don't let her stay in too long."

"I won't."

"How much do I owe you for the magazines?"

"Not to worry."

"Well, then, the room is gratis."

That was fair. He felt a bit better.

At the Bath a white-costumed woman showed him and the little girl into a bathroom of their own. She unveiled the child and made no comment at the sores running over her tummy and back. As she dipped the child into the waters an unholy noise bounded across the room, beating against the tile, skating the surface of the waters, testing the room's closeness. "Nein! Nein!" the little girl screamed over and over again. The salesman had to cover his ears.

The waters did not bubble or churn; there was nothing to be afraid of. The salesman finally found his tongue. "What is the matter, sweetheart? You never feel water touch your skin before this?"

But the child said nothing in response, only took some gasps of breath, and suddenly he felt like a thief, not the savior he preferred.

"Nein! Nein!" she started up again, and the woman in white put her hand over his treasure's mouth, clamping it tight and holding her down in the temperate waters rising up from the karst.

She held her down the requisite fifteen minutes and then lifted her out, shaking her slightly, drying her, and only two bright tears were left, one on each cheek, and he knew if he got close enough, he would be reflected in them.

The woman swaddled the child in a white towel, saying, "No need to return this." She glanced back, in wonder he was sure, then turned the knob and was gone.

If the waters were as magic as promised, maybe he would not have to return. He lifted the little girl up in his arms and felt a sharp sensation as she sank her baby teeth into his cheek, drawing blood.

*   *   *

The salesman had tied the stack of *Jets* tightly, and Rosalind had to work the knife under the string, taking care not to damage the cover of the magazine on top. The string gave way and the stack slid apart. The faces of Jackie Wilson, Sugar Ray Robinson, and Dorothy Dandridge glanced up at her. A banner across one cover read EMMETT TILL, THE STORY INSIDE. She arranged herself on a wicker chaise on the verandah and began her return to the world she'd left behind.

She took the photographs — there were photographs — released by his mother — he was an only child — his mother was a widow — he stuttered — badly — these were some details — she took the photographs into her — into herself — and she would never let them go.

She would burn the magazine out back with the kitchen trash — drop it in a steel drum and watch the images curl and melt against turtle shell — she'd give the other magazines to Hamlet as she always did — he had a scrapbook of movie stars and prize fighters and jazz musicians.

The mother had insisted on the pictures, so said *Jet*. This is my son. Swollen by the beating — by the waters of the River Pearl — misshapen — unrecognizable — monstrous.

Hamlet heard her soft cries out in the kitchen, over the steam of turtle meat.

"Missis is all right?"

She made no answer to his question, only waved him off with one hand, the other covering the black and white likeness of the corpse. She did not want Hamlet to see where she came from.

America's waterways.

She left the verandah and went out back.

Blood trickled from the salesman's cheek.

"Is vampire you vampire, sweetheart?"

"What are you telling me?"

They were sitting on the verandah after dinner, the tourists having strolled to Milk River, guided by Hamlet, to watch the crocodiles in the moonlight.

"Are they man-eaters? Are they dangerous?" one tourist woman inquired.

"They are more afraid of you than you could possibly be of them," Hamlet told her.

The little sharp-toothed treasure was swaddled in the towel from the Bath and curled up on a chaise next to Rosalind. Tomorrow the salesman would have to buy her decent clothes.

If he decided to keep her.

But he must keep her.

"I gave a woman twenty American dollars for her."

"What is she?"

What indeed, this blond and blue-eyed thing, filled with vanilla ice cream, bathing in the moonlight that swept the verandah.

Not a hot moon tonight. Not at all.

He rubbed his cheek where the blood had dried.

"Her people came from overseas, long time ago."

They sat in the quiet, except for the backnoise of the tropics. As if unaware of any strangeness around them.

Silence.

His wife would never stand for it.

He might keep his treasure here. He would pay her room and board, collect her on his travels. A lot of men had outside children. He would keep in touch with his.

Why was he such a damn coward?

Rosalind would never agree to such a scheme, that he knew.

But no harm in asking.

It would have to wait. He'd sleep on it.

But when he woke, all he woke to was a sharp pain in his cheek. He touched the place where the pain seemed keenest and felt a round hardness that did not soften to his touch but sent sharp sensations clear into his eyes.

When he raised his eyelids, the room was a blur. He waited for his vision to clear but nothing came. The red hatband was out of sight.

He felt the place in the bed where his treasure had slept. There was a damp circle on the sheet. She was gone.

monster

MY GRANDMOTHER's house. Small. In the middle of nowhere. The heart of the country, as she is the heart of the
country. Mountainous, dark, fertile.

One starting point.

My grandmother's house is electrified in the sixties.
Nothing fancy. No appliances. A couple of bare light bulbs
sway on black queues in the parlor, dining room, cast a
glare across the verandah, cutting moonlight. Now scrip-
ture can be read at all hours, no fear of damaging eyes.

There are two pictures on the walls of the parlor. Two
photographs, hung so high the images are out of reach,
distorted as they rest against the molding, slanting down-
ward. Her two living sons. Each combed and slicked to
resemble a forties movie star. The one with the blue-black
hair and widow's peak thinks he favors Robert Taylor. This
alone will draw the girls to him, he thinks, somewhere
back in time.

Today he is bald and rubs guano into his scalp over
morning coffee to ignite the follicles. His wife belches

loudly and slaps her feet across the tile floor, her soles as wide as a gravedigger's shovel.

Pictures taken in a studio in downtown Kingston, where touched-up brides (lightened to reflect the island obsession) grace the window.

My grandmother's faith is severe and forbids graven images (she makes an exception for her sons), dancing, smoking, drinking (except for the blood of the Lamb, bottled and shipped from another end of the Empire).

Does she look the other way when her boys take a dark girl into the bush? Does she object? I have no way of knowing and wouldn't dare to ask.

Graven images include motion pictures, of course. Although she has never seen a movie, she has seen advertisements for them in the *Daily Gleaner*, right next to the race results. Nasty things.

Like most evil, brought from elsewhere.

My father loves the movies to death, as do I. Some of our best times are spent in the dark, thrilled by the certainty that in the dark anything can happen. It's out of our control. The screen says: Sit back and enjoy the show!

We lived some of my childhood in New York City, visiting Jamaica once or twice a year, down the way where the nights are gay and the sun shines daily on the mountaintop. These were the fifties, sixties. In the City we go (at least) twice a week to the local movie house, the St. George, where we escape, comforted by the smell of popcorn mingling with disinfectant.

We are comforted also by the name. We live in America, as we will always call it, but are children of the Empire. St. George is our patron, his cross our standard. We are triangular people, our feet on three islands.

The interior of the movie house is overwhelmingly red, imaging Seville, Granada. The St. George sports no dragon, no maiden chained to a rock, no knight in shining armor, but is decorated as if a picture book of Spain sometime after 1492. A *trompe l'oeil* bullfighter makes a pass outside the men's room. Señoritas with mantillas and filigreed fans hang above our seats, gossiping across wrought iron balconies, *duenna* watchful.

Built in the heyday of the movie palaces, the delicacy of the Alhambra arches across the screen; whose dream was this?

"Someday, Rachel, someday, when we're long gone and people, archaeologists, dig this up, like Schliemann at Troy, they'll think it was one of our cathedrals. You mark my words."

Against his projection of the future our timespans come together; the barest ellipse separates us. We're practically contemporaries. "When we're long gone." Imagine saying that to a child.

"Our lives are written in disappearing ink."

I lie awake, terrified.

I am about nine or ten, but I know all about Schliemann and the four levels of Troy; in the time before the theater darkens my father instructs me in things that fascinate him. Victoriana. The ripping. "From crotch to crown, my dear, from crotch to crown."

When the chandelier in the ceiling begins to blink off and on, signifying the start of the show, we fall into silence.

We prefer mysteries, war movies, westerns. Love stories and musicals are for girls. Like my mother, who never joins us in the dark.

Science fiction is our absolute favorite, with horror close behind. The disembodied hands. The Man with the X-ray Eyes.

THEM!

The redness of the Forbidden Planet.

"You must make allowances for my daughter, gentlemen. She's never known another human being except her father."

At night all hell breaks loose.

"What do you think they eat, Rachel?"

"Vienna sausage and asparagus straight from the can," I respond with my favorites.

We dare each other to eat raw meat, "like cannibals," he says. Slice the muscle that protects the littleneck and devour him whole, "in one gulp."

In my mind my father and the movies will be forever joined. Dana Andrews in the Flying Fortress graveyard. The decorated boy.

My father found himself in the Army Air Corps of the U.S.A. They filled his teeth with Carborundum, something to do with nonpressurized planes. Up there, in the wild blue yonder, flying high into the sun, he heard music in his head and thought he'd been shot down and gone to heaven, until, and this is a true story, until he heard, "Oh, Rochester."

"Coming, Mr. Benny."

And he realized that it hadn't been an angel singing but Dennis Day, the Irish tenor on *The Jack Benny Show,* and my father's teeth were behaving like a Philco, as he told the story.

My father would like to be an exception, like my grandmother's sons, and hang in the parlor on high.

My father tries to tell her that Cecil B. DeMille's *Ten Commandments* is a work of devotion and respect and could be used in Sunday school to illustrate the wonders of God.

She only smiles.

As if to say, when you need a graven image to perceive the glory of God, you're as bad as Aaron and them who worshipped the golden calf. As if to say, when your people were running fire through the canefields, I was cutting cane.

She doesn't even have a cross in her house. Jesus is in her heart. Is he Black in there?

When she dreams of him, who does he favor?

I don't know why she agreed to it, probably for the sake of her daughter, but on a Boxing Day — called by some "*their* Christmas" in answer to the childish question "How come Lillian isn't with her children today?" "Don't fret; Boxing Day is their Christmas." — anyway, on a Boxing

Day in the seventies, the last time I was on the island, she allowed my father to show a movie, casting the images on a white sheet spread across the verandah, straining the Delco almost to the point of collapse.

She sits on the verandah behind the sheet, to the side of the mouth of the parlor. Night begins to come on, she rocks.

The people in the surrounding area look to her for judgment, guidance, the food she generously gives them, and if she has let her big, strong, American-sounding son-in-law bring a movie to them, how can it be wrong?

At dusk they begin arriving. Trudging up the red clay hill (vainly assayed for alumina by my uncles), dressed in almost all white are the women, looking as if they are headed for a full immersion baptism.

They come out of curiosity, respect, but not all are convinced of the rightness of the occasion. Some of the women nestle asafoetida bags between their breasts, just in case; acridity rises in the heat, damp from Christmas fat (as December rain is known) of the evening. A woman in the line has sewn pockets into her Sea Island cotton underpants, in which she places chestnuts, one in each pocket, so when he sleeps with her tonight, her husband will not impregnate her.

My father has planned the evening carefully. He is ringmaster, magician, the author of adventure. He is eager, nervous. He is to reveal the world beyond their world — of red dirt which sticks in every human crevice; teeth darkened by cane, loosened in the dark; eye-whites reddened by smoke, rum. He wants to become crucial to them.

He's lost interest in me, given me up. He began to lose interest in me when I grew breasts, kept secrets in a diary, bled. Not an unfamiliar story, I imagine. He tried to harness me, driven to extremes that I now regard as pathetic, but then — then I recalled the reins they held me by when I was two, three. He eventually realized it was no use, but not without World War III.

Still, I was there that evening. The last time I spent on the island.

Before the picture show there is a short display of fireworks. A taste of magic, unfamiliar, before the greater magic. Fireworks bought from a Chinese shopkeeper, a man from Shanghai, for whom there wasn't enough room in Hong Kong. Bought behind colored strands masking the storeroom in the Paradise Lost & Found. The island is ripe for explosion, people crave gunpowder. But for American currency, caution is suspended.

The sky lowers over us, black. The promise of magic is everywhere, natural, unnatural. Magicians, natural, unnatural. The woman with chestnuts in her drawers. My father, a pint of Myers' in his back pocket.

An Otaheite tree hosts the sputtering end of a St. Catherine's wheel.

The sputtering wheel is the only light but for the bulb of the projector. My father threads the film, fitting into the sprockets the Hollywood version of *Frankenstein*. One of the greatest movies ever made, he tells them, a classic like the book, he says, written by the wife of Percy Bysshe Shelley, the great Romantic poet.

"Me preffer Byron," a voice breaks in.

My father makes no sign that he has heard.

It could be worse, will be with any luck.

"Me preffer McKay."

"Me preffer Salkey."

"Me preffer Mikey Smith."

"Me seh me cyaan believe it."

My father doesn't mention that the author of *Franken-stein,* since we're identifying her through family ties, was the daughter of Mary Wollstonecraft.

The night is alive with the scent of women. Asafoetida. Sweat. The ash of St. Catherine. Talcum powder.

My father wouldn't know Mary Wollstonecraft from Virginia Woolf, nor know they had more in common than some stones in their pockets, nor know the significance of stones, nor care.

Shelley is far more to the point. They have memorized "Ozymandias" in school. Most of them. Or had their knuckles split across. Their own people came from an antique land.

Most of the ships landed no more than fifty miles from here, in either direction.

The sound of the projector. A soft rattle across toads, insects. Night-flyers. A family of croakers, somewhere ghost-white in the middle of the night. Lizards who mate for life and walk upside-down on ceilings, sucking the whitewashed plaster to their feet. Moon rises, grazing the screen. The doctor throws the switch. Caliban stirs. Peenie-wallies are attracted, their luminescent ends flashing past the black-and-white.

My grandmother's shade.

I use the light cast from the projector, the images on the sheet, the lurching monster, to glance across the audience.

On a girl apart from the group, unto herself, is an ancient dress of mine. What was once called polished cotton, blue with a pink rose in the center of the bodice, pink streamers sewn at the neck cascade down the wearer's back. Colors faded to paleness by now, from sun, riverwater, the battery of women against rock. I remember trying it on in a dressing room in Lord & Taylor. I must have been about eleven, worried about what I'd heard in the girls' bathroom, that department store dressing rooms were equipped with two-way mirrors. Right now a stranger was scanning me, my undeveloped chest, panties, baby fat. I got to wear it for Easter Sunday. Now it reappears on the body of the daughter of the butcher's wife, apart from the group. Reddish skin. Almond-shaped green eyes.

Her eyes could make her my sister. Stranger things have happened. It is not uncommon here to be strolling down a dirt road and come up against someone who is your "dead stamp."

While I stare at this girl, while the gathered company watches the progress of the monster, a Roman candle has settled into an eave on the roof of the house, nestling between the mahogany shingles. Slowly the fire takes root. Slowly at first, then gathering frequency and height, sparks shoot into the night sky and fall dying on our shoulders like shooting stars.

Bats fly from under the peak of the roof, screaming as one, furious.

The monster is talking to a little girl at the side of a lake.

FIRE! someone finally yells.

The little girl is gone.

My father is wild.

"Rachel, take over!" he shouts, as if he still trusts me, then runs toward the house.

"Whatever happens, don't stop the movie!" He shouts back to me as he runs.

The mob is chasing the monster by firelight, torches raised above their heads, as sparks cascade across the sheet, across my grandmother's silhouette, and the bats make another pass, demanding attention.

No one moves. This is not their house. No one stops watching.

Poor lickle white child.

Is what happen?

Him nuh kill she?

My father has vaulted onto the roof, is stamping out God's wrath with his tenderized American feet.

contagious melancholia

"DID YOU NOTICE they didn't even have a piece of evergreen tacked to the walls?"

"Poor devils."

My parents, sitting in the front seat of the Vauxhall, are reminiscing about a visit just completed, to the house where an old family friend, Miss Small, and her invalid sister live. We visit them only on Christmas, the most exciting day of the year for the likes of us. We recognize how fortunate we are.

"How the mighty are fallen." In this sliver of the island such language applies.

Almost the same exact exchange takes place year after year, followed by a recitation of the vast holdings once enjoyed by the Smalls, where there are now developments, hotels, alumina operations. And the Smalls realized little profit, the fault of an outsider who mismanaged the properties. There are a thousand such stories on this island; my father seems to know them all.

Miss Small is called by her family (none left but the sister) and friends (which you can count on one hand, so few remain) Girlie. She lives up to her name.

She is tiny in stature, each year growing smaller. At eleven I overwhelm her in height. She is dressed this particular Christmas Day in what looks to be an old school uniform, down to the striped tie and tied-up brown oxfords. She wears tortoiseshell spectacles. The huge, seagoing ancient beasts are an island treasure. We do not worship them, as did the Arawak; but we know they are worth a lot. Their shells are sold for eyeglass frames, their flesh for tinned soup. I drank them once in the Place de l'Odéon in Paris.

Miss Small's chestnut hair is bobbed and turns under at her neckline. The spectacles make her eyes big, two surprised circles, dark brown, against a pallid, lineless skin.

Her girlishness seems intact. She claps her hands in excitement when my father presents her with a tin of Huntley & Palmer's Christmas assortment.

As we enter the house the wireless is tuned to the Queen's message, coming to us live from what my father calls the Untidy Kingdom. He believes this puts them in their place, as when he refers to our neighbor to the north as the Untidy Snakes of America.

We sometimes live in New York City but always return home.

One return took place a week after Emmett Till's body was found. I heard my mother behind their bedroom door, "I've had enough of this damn-blasted place!"

That's another story.

✴   ✴   ✴

I have never seen Miss Small's sister, Miriam. I have only heard her voice, calling from the room where she is bed-ridden. When I ask what is wrong with her, why doesn't she get up, my mother demurs, muttering something about "disappointment."

"What kind of disappointment?" I ask, hoping for a true-romance response. At best a fiancé killed in a war; at least an outside child.

"In life," my mother sighs.

In a few days, believe it or not, only ninety miles away, on another island, where turtles were also worshipped, the rebel forces are to take Havana.

"Rachel, go into the kitchen with Miss Girlie and see if you can be of help."

I follow my tiny host down the hall to the back of the house, to the kitchen, where my eyes are met with an excitement of roaches, another huge and ancient beast known to us. They scramble across a mound of wet sugar someone has spilled on a counter.

"Bitches," Girlie mutters under her breath. I do not know if she refers to the cockroaches, who know no shame, continuing to scramble over the mound, their feet gloriously crystalline with sugar, even after she has flat-tened one with a teacup, or does she mean the two women who are visible to me through the slats in the jalousie window.

"Pardon, Miss Girlie?" I say, not quite believing a word

she would never utter in the parlor has escaped her mouth in the kitchen.

"Nothing."

The two women are no longer in my line of vision.

The remains of the cockroach cling to the bottom of the teacup in her hand.

The sugar mound appears to be the only food in sight. The safe, as it's called, a screen-fronted cabinet designed to stay flies and roaches, stands before me, apparently empty, not even a tin of sardines.

She catches me looking.

"Damn bitches nuh tek all me foodstuff?" She speaks for them to understand.

Cigarette smoke rises outside the jalousie. Someone is listening.

"Listen to de bitch, nuh. Listen to she. Nasty man-woman."

Miss Girlie gives a little shrug and places the teacup on a tray.

"Shouldn't we rinse it off?"

She nods and hands the cup to me. I turn on the tap. Nothing.

"You will have to use the standpipe in the yard. This tap does not function at the moment."

I find an enamel pan to catch water and head out back. I know my entry into the yard will cause comment. We live in an oral society in which everything, every move, motion, eyeflash, is commented upon, catalogued, categorized, approved or disapproved. The members of this society are my writing teachers, but I don't know this yet.

The two women wear the dark blue dresses and white aprons usual to Kingston maids. I don't know their names. We visit only once a year, and the personnel is never the same.

"You raise where?" I am immediately spoken to.

"Pardon?"

"Me say is where dem raise you?"

"Why?"

"Far me wish fi know why you nuh wish we a Happy Christmas?"

"Happy Christmas, missis."

"You hear de chile? Is too late fe dat. Better watch de man-woman nuh get she."

I am reddening, which will cause more comment. About the resemblance my skin bears to a pig, for one thing.

I am too young to understand it.

I bend over the standpipe and pray that the trickle soon fills the enamel pan. I have set the teacup to one side.

"Me name Patsy." The second woman is speaking to me.

"Happy Christmas, Patsy."

"Change a come."

I slowly rinse the cockroach shell and guts from the flowered cup.

"Me say change a come. It due."

"Lord Jesus," the woman who is not Patsy is speaking.

"Missis?"

"Is what dat on de teacup?"

"Cockroach."

"Lord Jesus, what a nasty smaddy."

Back in the kitchen Girlie is standing in a corner, her eyes focused on the floor.

"I must make some tea for Miriam, my sister," she says.

"Where is the tea?" I ask her.

"In the safe."

I open the door into the emptiness, and with great care, and certain knowledge my hand is about to encounter something truly dreadful, feel around for Earl Grey or lapsang souchong. Something wet is on my finger; I quickly draw it back. Without looking I wipe my hand on my best clothes. Another foray into the darkness of the safe and I manage to find an envelope with the words "Tower Isle Hotel" stamped on it. Inside there is a handful of miserable leaves.

"Miss Girlie, where is the teapot?"

"In the breakfront in the drawing room. I will fetch it."

I know I must venture again into the yard to fetch water for the tea.

The woman who is not Patsy has left. Patsy has her back against the wall of the house, one leg bent for balance, the foot flat against grayish wood.

She is staring into space.

"I'm just here to get some more water."

"Please yourself."

The yard is the classic design of old-style Kingston houses. A verandah attached to the kitchen overlooks a rectangular space, across which are the servants' quarters. Invariably thin rooms with one square of window.

I am brought up not to think about such things, to be content with paradise.

There is something about Patsy as she stands against that wall, her foot bent back like a great sea bird. I say this now, describing her image in my brain. But then? Then I was probably glad of the quiet, of the absence of the other woman, her tongue.

The water trickles into the enamel pan, finally filling it. I return to the kitchen.

Miss Girlie awaits, with a flowered teapot, a riot of pansies and forget-me-nots fading with time and the hard water of Kingston. I take the pot from her and put the measly handful of leaves into the stained inside. She puts the water on the kerosene stove.

Who were the Misses Small? For these are real women I have been talking about. Down to their names. They are long gone. Girlhood chums of my great-grandmother, they cluster together in my mind with all the other mad, crazy, eccentric, disappointed, demented, neurasthenic women of my childhood, where Bertha Mason grew on trees. Every family of our ilk, every single one, had such a member. And she was always hidden, and she was always a shame, and she was always the bearer of that which lay behind us.

part two

....

down the shore

NEPTUNE. LONG BRANCH. Navesink. Sea Girt. Manas-
quan. Atlantic Highlands.

Pinball. Boardwalks. Salt-water taffy.

"Don't dwell on the past so."

Cabins in a rectangle. Wading pool in the center. Knotty
pine inside a cabin. Lying on a cot, a girl can't sleep; she is
counting the knots. The pine smell is overwhelming. She
gets no comfort from it. She connects it to the disinfectant
they use at school. What is happening, has happened?

What is she wearing?

Why can't she sleep?

Where are the grown-ups?

Getting loaded?

Fighting?

Maybe she's not alone?

Driving past such a place thirty years and thousands of
miles later, she feels a sudden dreadfulness.

"Don't dwell on the past so."

Outside STEAKS & CHOPS is flashing red/dark,

red/dark. She tries counting the flashes on and off, on and off, but nothing works. She is wide awake.

Across the shore road. SEAFOOD. COCKTAILS.

Thirty years and thousands of miles later, a picture forms in her mind.

Those glass cases in the front of restaurants. After-dinner mints.

But mostly cigars.

Cigarettes are dispensed from mirrored machines in which women check if their lipstick needs repair, has smeared their front teeth.

The funny house mirror in Asbury Park. Someone is giving her a quarter so she can see herself. The elongation of her; her body is waves. She is fluid, unsound. She could melt away.

Crimson cigarette ends die in clear glass ashtrays imprinted with a fisherman in a slicker. ORIGINAL HOUSE OF SEAFOOD. She can make out a sharp edge.

She sees a woman she recognizes at the table. A Kool lazing in the ashtray, ashening the fisherman's beard.

The woman is talking to someone.

The girl can't make out who it is.

Remember, this is thirty years and thousands of miles later. She is dwelling on the past; she has no choice.

None.

Cigar boxes embossed with exotic-looking women, or feathered savages, welcoming the after-dinner man to the pleasures of a smoke.

Hav-A-Tampa. Muriel.

"Why don't you pick me up and smoke me sometime?"

She is seven or eight or nine and peering into one of those cases. The woman with Kool has her by the hand. The woman is paying the cashier.

"I wonder how many of these you sell?" The woman indicates the Mason Mint in her hand.

The cashier smiles.

The picture is crystal.

It could shatter.

In the cabin the woman is nowhere to be seen.

Thirty years and thousands of miles later she feels like the girl in the Ringling Brothers sideshow her grandmother took her to. No arms or legs; a pen in her mouth. Her autograph. She has a pen in her mouth.

She is wetting the bed.

"Have this; it'll take the taste away."

The girl unwraps the sphere carefully and takes delicate bites from the Mason Mint. She folds the foil with care and puts it in her pajama pocket. The pj's are flannel, soft from many washings, with pink creatures dancing over them.

Thirty years and thousands of miles later a friend is saying she just assumed children had lousy memories.

That's how she's always felt. She can reconstruct the sixteenth century better than her own life.

the store of a million items

AS CHILDREN WE HAD our seasons, apart from grown-up, growing seasons. Our own ways of dividing time, managing the elliptical motion of the Earth, life on a spinning planet. Our ways were grounded, uncelestial. Light years were beyond us; black holes not yet imagined. Our idea of a matter-destroying entity was the sewer under the city, stygian, dripping, where Floridian Godzillas survived on Norwegian rats.

No, our seasons were set by the appearance of something in The Store of a Million Items, on Victory Boulevard, between the Mercury Cleaners and the Mill End Shop. The store was a postwar phenomenon, promising a bounty only available in America. Everything we loved was there; there we flocked. As close to infinity as we dared.

The first Duncan yo-yo — the first to catch the eye, splendid, gold-flecked, *deluxe,* guaranteed to go around the world, without end, singing all the while — usually appeared sometime in March, brought by common carrier from the Midwest. It led the way, grand marshal of a parade of yo-yos, lined up in a corner of the store window, as less *deluxe*, less articulate yo-yos followed, right down to the 29¢ model, thick wood and flaccid kitchen string, unable to sleep or sing, promising no momentum at all. Its brand-new cherry-red face was deceptively bright, for the paint would soon enough crack, strip, even run in the rain, dyeing its master, mistress red-handed. Stamped MADE IN JAPAN, which phrase then signified nothing so much as inferiority, cheapness. The work of the un-American.

But — and this is important, the teacher stressed — you couldn't trust MADE IN USA either, for right after Hiroshima, a Japanese town had changed its name to USA (pronounced you-sah) and therefore MADE IN USA was suspect. The un-American was crafty.

"Too many people don't understand Hiroshima," Miss Clausen continued. "Make sure it's U-period, S-period, A-period," she cautioned.

Yet the child who couldn't afford a grander, made in U-period, S-period, A-period yo-yo (and was too chicken, or good, to lift one) would treasure even the Japanese version, determined to overcome its birthright and teach it to sleep. Fingering the wood in his pants pocket, rubbing it along the wale of her corduroy skirt, you could hear the call of the schoolyard, while the teacher's voice became white noise.

We stood in clusters on the concrete, surrounded by the whirr of yo-yos sleeping. In the shape of the world, the world on a string.

We were truly blessed, the principal assured us.

Behind the Iron Curtain were streets of empty markets, with nothing but shelf after shelf of noodles. That's what happened when people lived on handouts. Everybody had cardboard in their shoes, not just the poor kids or the kids whose parents had better use for their money. Behind the Iron Curtain they sold *Uncle Tom's Cabin,* stamped 1955, with the words "first edition" on the title page.

We knew better.

On August 28, 1955, Emmett Till's body was dredged from the River Pearl. But teachers weren't responsible for telling us about things that happened in summer.

Behind the Iron Curtain everything was gray — people, cities, skies. The sun didn't shine there. They were deprived of Happy Tooth, while Mr. Tooth Decay dogged their tracks, like a villain in a silent two-reeler. Even the children had false teeth, if they were lucky.

In 1956 we passed around a special edition of *Life* devoted to the Hungarian Revolution. We were about to receive a refugee classmate. Some of us were foreign-born, but he would be our first refugee. Gray tanks rumbled through streets page after page. People were squashed. For some reason the refugee went to Chicago instead.

The years moved on. Jacks. Marbles. Jump ropes. Pea shooters.

Water pistols. My personal favorite. Coming at the end of spring, the verge of summer vacation, when we watched the green canvas shade, drawn down against the sun and against our eyes, drawn by the warmth of the outdoors, trained on long evenings. The shade flapped gently, but any breeze was trapped.

Black lugers. Silver derringers. Translucent ray guns. One blast and your enemy would disintegrate before your very eyes. We'd all seen *The Day the Earth Stood Still. The Thing. It Came from Outer Space.* Pods landing in a California valley.

Earth Versus the Flying Saucers.

"Will they be back, Brad?"

"Not as long as we're here, Sally."

Saturday mornings in the children's pit of the local movie house, the matron, whom some of us would come to remember as a stone butch, patrolled the aisles during the show. She collected water pistols at the door, those she could detect, or tried to remember the children who were likely to be armed.

We hated her with a feeling as natural as what we felt for Messala in *Ben Hur.*

"C'mon, Ben!" we cheered during the chariot race and thrilled as Ben's nemesis was dragged bloody through the sand of the Circus Maximus.

Of course some of us eluded the matron's once-over and we blasted her again and again, water running over her ducktail, droplets bouncing off her Vitalis'ed strands, soaking the nurse's uniform they dressed her in.

"Bas-tuds!" She swore at us, calling us chicken, threatening to stop the picture and raise the lights.

When the water ran out, we pelted her with Goobers and Raisinets, Good-and-Plenty, and Milk Duds.

Then she brought out the heavy artillery, the ticket-taker, for one final warning: "Now, boys and girls." To which we either feigned good behavior or began a rampage, depending on whether we knew the ending of the movie or cared. We were in that dark pit gloriously leaderless. Anarchy for the most part prevailed.

In school we declared War! (what else?) on each other. The-girls-against-the-boys, the-boys-against-the-girls, ancient compound nouns, spoken in one rapid breath, running back and forth during recess, reloading our sidearms in the girls' room, the boys' room. There was a rumor a boy in 5–3 peed in his.

Even Gerald O'Brien who draped pop beads from The Store of a Million Items around his waist and pretended he was a mermaid — like Ann Blyth, he said — armed himself. Gerald wouldn't have been caught dead at the movies on Saturday morning. He said he preferred solitude, hated crowds, and watched his movies in peace on *The Early Show,* in the time between the end of school and his parents' return from work. He drank tap water from a stemmed glass he'd bought in The Store of a Million Items, into which he dropped two cocktail onions, calling himself a Gibson Girl. He would have preferred to have used his water pistol as a prop in high drama or melodrama, *The Letter* or *Deception,* the first frames of *Mildred Pierce,* the final scene of *Duel in the Sun,* not as the rest of us did, in gross displays of force.

"Boys and girls, boys and girls, hold your partner's hand," we were told, as we were marched from one place to another, to the schoolyard, gym, auditorium for assembly on Friday mornings, to the lunchroom, which always smelled of alphabet soup no matter the entree of the day.

Seated in front of a plate on which sugary Franco-American ravioli and sauce has congealed, a girl suddenly pulls a derringer from a pleat in her plaid skirt and lays waste to her lunch partner.

"Drop it!" The lunch marshal swoops into action, confiscating the gun, huge tins (fallout shelter size) of cling peaches bearing witness on a shelf behind her, SCIENTIA EST POTENTIA etched in tile above her head.

A visit to the Brooklyn Botanical Gardens, where exotica have been gathered, labeled, staked. Where armed children descend in the glass-enclosed re-creation of a tropical rain forest, heavy mist thickening with their excited breath, the City's rising humidity. We are running, tripping over metal stakes, tags identifying tree ferns, bromeliads, orchids, flesh wet with scent, the place as lush as the Hanging Gardens of Babylon, which we've memorized as one of the Seven Wonders of the Ancient World and can only imagine.

The tropics have seized us. The teachers have not seen anything like it since some seventh-graders escaped from the star show at the Hayden Planetarium and occupied the war canoe at the Museum of Natural History.

They scream for order.

"Hey, Jesse, this make you homesick for Puerto Rico?"

Does he mean the chaos or the foliage?

"Man, you don't know nothing."

"I like to be in America . . ."

The guerrillas are swarming. Thin streams from our pistols whip the mist further. We have created our own fog. A wall lies ahead of us.

Someone, off by himself, hidden, is tracing in the glass of the greenhouse: VITO WAS HERE.

The steam will dissipate, the letters disappear.

"Death doesn't make sense in summer," one girl tells another. "Last summer, when Marilyn Monroe died, I just didn't get it."

"Yeah."

"Maybe it's not summer. Maybe it was being at camp. You don't expect bad things to happen."

"Yeah."

There was a vacant lot about two blocks up the hill from school. Traces of a former structure could be detected in the ground, but what dominated the lot and drew some of us into it were several huge boulders we named the Mexican Rocks, lending the exotic, the untamed, to a common urban terrain, making it strange.

One day Gerald O'Brien is taking a shortcut from school to *The Early Show* through the vacant lot. He hears a moan, then the sound of something scraping against rock, the granite which is the bedrock of the island. He looks into the bushes. Suddenly he is afraid of what he will find. He sees the thin arm of a girl, charm bracelet dragging in the dirt. Zodiacal fishes, Eiffel Tower, Statue of

Liberty, Sacred Heart, each displayed in clear plastic trays at The Store of a Million Items, are visible, beside the bulk of a man in a business suit, who is moaning. Gerald wishes he were in The Store of a Million Items right now, browsing.

Or at home, in front of his flickering images, hearing "The Syncopated Clock," heralding *The Early Show.*

"Hey, mister! Quit it, mister! Quit it!" He screams at the back of the man.

"You wanna crush her?!"

The man doesn't seem to hear him.

Gerald picks up a discarded Pepsi bottle and, knowing only he wants this to stop, shuts his eyes and cracks the man on the back of the head.

"What the fuck?!"

Gerald has the man's attention. He moves back a few steps, afraid of what is coming next. "Oh, shit," the man says, under his breath, as if this were nothing.

He gets up and begins to walk away, down the hill toward the schoolyard, brushing his suit as he goes.

The girl just lies there, uncovered, her plaid skirt up, bright red stains her upper leg. Gerald is afraid to touch her. He lays his pullover over her. The wool scratches her. She starts; cries. "Stay here," he says.

"Please; don't leave me."

He sits with her until another grown-up comes by, a woman loaded down with groceries. He does his best to tell the woman what happened. He stares at the ACME stamped on her bags as he speaks.

"Why, you're a little hero," she says.

Gerald is commended at the next assembly. He never sees the girl again. No one does. She disappears down the Jersey shore with her mother and father, who pray it will not follow them. Gerald's father tries to reconcile his pansy of a son with the hero of the Mexican Rocks.

The PTA chips in and buys Gerald a glove embossed with Mickey Mantle's signature.

At The Store of a Million Items baseball gloves, cards, bats, balls, caps give way. School approaches. Marbled notebooks, Crayolas, pencil cases, rulers, erasers, compasses, protractors, things vital and unnecessary lie side by side under BACK TO SCHOOL.

Time passes. Seasons change.

Soon enough it is nearing Christmas and "Silver Bells" is piped to the sidewalk from The Store of a Million Items. We're getting in the mood. We watch as a whole window is cleared for the Flexible Flyers — surely the most beautiful name anything was ever given. They are arranged like fallen dominoes, one resting against the next, Eagle trademark echoing behind the glass.

There is a loud explosion. A huge clap over the City.

A fireball follows, rolling in the early dark of the December afternoon, above the last-minute shoppers, the schoolchildren looking to the holiday. Some of us think: "Russia," "Communism," "Sneak attack." We duck and cover and wait for the all-clear.

There is no sound.

Outside it begins to rain people. Arms and legs catch in the ailanthus, the ginkgo trees. Torsos bounce from awnings. Scraps of metal shine through the slush. Airsick bags dissolve in the streets. Samsonite jams a storm drain. It's unbelievable.

No one will forget it. Nobody doesn't talk about it. I heard this, I heard that. In the halls, on the line in the lunchroom, over trays heavy with Weissglass milk and Dinty Moore beef stew. "I seen a head rolling to the Colonial Lanes."

"You're full of it."

"My mom's a nurse. You probably wouldn't believe her neither. She said they had to put the pieces together, just so's they could bury them. There must have been millions of pieces, she said."

"I bet."

"She said you couldn't tell if they were a man or a woman, or colored neither."

That gets someone's attention.

"Isn't that a sin?"

"What?"

"To bury people all mixed up."

"I guess."

A woman on the radio says she dreamed it before it happened. "That's right. I dreamed there were sugar packets falling from the sky. Some said TWA, some said United. That's when I knew. I just didn't have the flight numbers."

"Have you had this . . ."

"Kind of experience before? You bet."

"They didn't know what hit them," is spoken all over the City as benediction.

The Store of a Million Items shifts the display of Flex-

ible Flyers, moves the mechanical Santa bowing to pas-
sers-by, cuts off "Silver Bells," and on snow made from
Ivory flakes, sets two black-shrouded model planes, as-
sembled by the owner's grandson.

The collision, the crash, the manmade thunder and
lightning, the rain of people, this was horrible enough,
and then came the news that a kid had caused it.

A girl and her father are sitting at a kitchen table. The
tabletop is Formica, gray with pink flamingos, covered
with a striped tablecloth. The table is a gift from generous
in-laws; the mother prefers the table covered. "No taste,"
her rationale.

The man is wearing a freshly laundered breakneck shirt,
his name embroidered over his left nipple. It's his bowling
night. He's taking time out to talk to his daughter.

"You know why those planes collided and all those people died?"

"No," she responds; but she does. The teacher told them
during current events that morning. Finding irresistible
the news that a boy playing with his transistor interfered
with the planes' communication with the tower at Idle-
wild and BOOM!

"What does that tell us, boys and girls?"

The girl knows her father wants to be the first to tell
her; so she lies, and feigns surprise as he gets to the point.

"A kid."

"I didn't know that." The woman at the sink, carefully
soaping the dinner plates, comments.

"Didn't you hear me?"

"Yes, Dad."

"Well?"

"You need help, Mom?"

"Stay put, young lady."

"Okay."

"Don't 'okay' me. I want you to hear this. A kid caused the whole thing."

"How?" She plays along.

"He was playing with his transistor, that's how."

Maybe it was hearing it a second time, being weary of the adult version, the blame attached to this dead boy. Maybe it was remembering Jesse Moreno whispering in her ear, "Better he shoulda been playing with himself." But a smile was starting and she was desperate to erase it.

Too late.

"You think that's funny?"

"No, Dad."

"Well, then. That's not all. You know what happened to him?"

"No."

"He landed a few blocks from his grandparents' house in Bay Ridge. He was visiting them for the holidays."

She is biting her bottom lip, hoping to bring on tears, avoid laughter. She hates crying in front of her parents but would welcome the embarrassment right now.

Her mother only makes it worse.

"What were his grandparents?"

"Catholic." He is adamant in his knowledge of these strangers.

"From Naples, originally."

"Poor things."

"Irony is what you call that."

"Honey?"

"What?"

"If they're all dead, how come we know this?"

"Know what?"

"That the boy caused the crash."

"The papers said he confessed before he died. Said he didn't listen to the stewardess when she asked him to stop. It was in all the papers."

"Poor thing."

"What poor thing? He took all those people with him. All because he wouldn't listen."

"Imagine how his people feel."

When we went with our mothers to buy shoes, in the back of The Store of a Million Items, the shoe salesman had us stand on a pair of metal feet and we were x-rayed. They thought they saw right through us, tissue, muscle, tendon became transparent and the bones beneath the skin, the skeleton of our feet was bared, cast in negative, like the Mr. Boneses hanging in the window around Halloween time.

stan's speed shop

"DON'T YOU THINK the sound of men's voices raised in harmony is a holy sound? You know, like the Beach Boys."

I was lying on the grass in the July sunlight, reading. The voice was coming from somewhere above my head.

My aunt had warned me that the son of a rich man she knew was crazy; although harmless, she insisted.

Once you're told someone is crazy, anything they say may be used to support the claim. Here was a case in point. His ecstatic question unsettled me.

I looked up. "Hello."

"Hi."

He was not dressed as another rich young man on a warm summer afternoon might be. He was wearing a khaki shirt and pants, and his hands shone with a film of oil. *Stan* was embroidered over one pocket of his shirt.

"I guess you've heard all about me."

I wasn't about to say. My aunt said the finest families had their skeletons. In some cases, she said, refinement existed in clear relation to strangeness. Look at our own family. We had enough skeletons to supply a medical school. Like a great uncle once incarcerated in New York City's Bellevue who kidnapped his nurse to the roof and suggested they take a lover's leap. The nurse said, "Oh, everyone jumps off the roof; let's go down and jump up."

Poor Uncle Billy. He fell for it.

We originated in the place where the sun never set and the blood never dried. Fragility was almost a point of honor, evidence of our delicacy against cruelty. Whatever happened, we weren't to blame, nor were we to make any change.

My aunt said that Stan was about twenty-five and that he chose to live in a room over the garage. In her words, "like a servant." Outside the windows to his room a sign hung, hand-lettered: STAN'S SPEED SHOP.

The shop was a space at the back of the six-car garage, decorated with girlie posters, calendars with half-naked women elongated against crushed satin backgrounds, their breasts as sharp as a medieval weapon. The girls hung from cords, above shelves of coolant and antifreeze, fan belts framing them on either side. There was a desk of sorts, with one of those spikes for impaling bills, and a glass ashtray from the Piping Rock Club.

"He's more to be pitied than censured," my aunt said. "Who in their right mind would think of looking for a car repair shop behind a great house on Long Island?"

"What are you reading?"

I held up my book for him to see.

"Oh, yeah, I heard about that one."

"It's very interesting." I was only twelve so a lot of *The Great Gatsby* was lost on me, but I liked what I could get out of it. Out of Gatsby especially. I had plans of escape. I kept a map of France over my bed and a jar where I saved money for my passage. I wanted to be different than the people I was related to. That meant breaking away.

"I guess I don't read much, except for car stuff. I hated school so I hate to read, except for car stuff."

I didn't mention that car stuff lay at the center of Fitzgerald's novel.

"I hate school too," I said, although I didn't.

He lowered himself to the ground beside me. "Okay?" he asked.

I nodded okay.

Then I sat up, keeping my finger in my place in the novel. Gatsby was about to pay the price. It was almost over.

Beyond the well-kept lawns on which we sat, and the crescent of a garden planted with strawberries and ancient roses, thick with time and scent, was the house, huge and brick, with only a suggestion of columns in front. Behind the house was the garage. Behind that were the tennis courts. And beyond them were the woods, which edged the property, which my aunt forbade me to explore. In the woods I could see an opening between trees, suggesting water. Without saying much my aunt allied the woods, and the water dividing them, with death and the maiden. I was properly frightened.

Stan and I and my aunt were the only residents at the moment except for a German couple who lived in and spoke only to each other.

Stan's mother was away for the summer, drying out in what my aunt referred to as a French hospital. Why I have no idea, except the word French attached itself to things one should be ashamed of; at least in our world. French letters, etc.

Stan's father was in Southeast Asia, protecting some investments against a possible coup.

I was there because my aunt was a friend of Stan's father and had been asked to look after things. That's what she told me. But there was really nothing to look after. The Germans saw to the house and grounds and Stan kept to himself and the family cars for the most part.

I did not suspect the real story until later that summer. In a letter from Stan's father saying he was going to be delayed "due to sudden unrest" was a check made out to my aunt, drawn on the Banque d'Indochine. Stan's father had written "companionship" in the space explaining the check. It was a nice touch.

I was acting as her beard.

The letter was as formal, as courtly as the check. The check was on heavy pale blue paper, the letter on thin hotel stationery. Each was scented with another time, a colonial grace note.

She had been sent here to wait on his return, whenever that happened, to catch some time with him before his nice dry wife reemerged. I didn't want to believe it was only a money arrangement, but maybe it was. The letter gave nothing away.

While she waited she did her best to entertain me. We went to Sagamore Hill, where she and I read the legends about Teddy Roosevelt. Looking back as I write this, I remember only a dark hall and a room filled with the heads of dead animals and their skins.

My aunt and I took our meals in the breakfast room, which looked out on a fish pond. Stan didn't eat with us. During the daytime he ate among the cars. In the evening he went into the village to a greasy spoon. My aunt and I had seen him there once. We were taking a stroll and spotted him from the back, hunched over the counter at the Kozy Korner.

"Poor devil," my aunt said, "like Montgomery Clift in *A Place in the Sun*. What's wrong with him, acting like a poor relation?"

"You said he was crazy," I reminded her.

"There's crazy and then there's crazy," she said, and I wasn't sure what she meant.

We walked on, away from the Kozy Korner, and turned toward what each of us had called "home" at least twice, when nothing could have been further from the truth.

When the German couple retired for the evening, my aunt and I explored the kitchen, which she called the "autopsy parlor."

"Why?" I asked her.

"All that stainless steel. Everything. Whoever heard of caging a light bulb? Like a bloody institution. From the refrigerators to the counters. I used to work in a hospital, you know."

I commented on the size of the two refrigerators. "Space for a few bodies," I said.

"They used to entertain a lot," my aunt said as she rummaged through bricks of dark chocolate, cracking one with a steel mallet, licking the crumbs from her hand, catching her face in the convex shine of steel. "Mind we leave things as we found them," she said, "or there will be hell to pay."

We tidied up the place, running a chamois over the steel counters.

"Those bloody Germans," she said as she switched off the light. "Bloody spies."

"Do you know who the aborigines are?"

"Yes."

My early schooling had been drenched in the repetitions of Empire. The aborigines lived in what Captain Cook had christened *terra nullius* — no man's land. The details were returning as they had been learned, in single file, by rote.

"I saw them once."

"How come?"

"My father had to go there on business. He took me along. It was long before now."

"Oh."

"Yeah. It's like the surface of Mars maybe."

I wasn't sure if this had anything to do with singing, with his original question.

"The dreams of the people. It's where the aborigines go to get away. Sometimes they sing the dreams. I was re-membering hearing them."

He started to get up. "Come with me to the garage. I want to show you something."

Every warning I'd ever been given about the danger of being female repeated itself. But I followed him anyway.

We walked through the side door out of the July sun. It was dark inside. I'd left my sandals on the grass along with *The Great Gatsby* and the concrete sent a chill up through me.

Stan switched on the lights. The cars were lit from above. A green-shaded hanging lamp cast its shadow across his desk.

"Wait'll you see this." He went over to the desk and pulled out a side drawer. "I got this on the same trip. We made a stop in South America. Do you know what it is?"

He thrust a small dark object toward me. "Look."

It was hard to make out the details of the thing in his hand, even with the lights on.

"Do you know what this is?"

"Not really."

He smiled. "It's a shrunken head, from up the Amazon. Scare you?"

Without a skull the head folded in on itself. That it once was attached to a human body was unbelievable.

The thing itself didn't frighten me.

"Look at the hair on this thing, the eyes." He swung the head back and forth in front of my face by its long lank hair.

"You're getting sleepy, very sleepy," he joked; I hoped. "When I snap my fingers your mind will go blank." Now he twisted the hair around his fist and thrust the head forward at me.

I backed up. "I better get going," I said, retreating further. "My aunt will be wondering where I am."

"Okey-dokey," he said and rocked back in his swivel chair. "Catch!"

The head made an arc toward me. I let it bounce off my chest where it hit, then turned and walked out of the garage. I shaded my eyes before I came into the brightness of the out of doors.

I was afraid he would come after me. In my mind's eye I was being dragged into the woods. But he didn't, and the last sound I heard from the garage was the noise of a car radio broadcasting a baseball game.

That night in the steel kitchen I wondered if I should tell my aunt what had happened.

She'd say I was lucky. It was my own fault for following a madman. Her declarations of his harmlessness would be forgotten. It was my fault and I was bloody lucky bloody worse did not transpire.

"What's that on your blouse?" she asked me under the steel-caged lights.

I looked down. There was a smudge where the head had made contact, a stain like chocolate. "Dirt, I guess."

"Well, leave it in the hamper for the German woman."

The German woman who did not speak to either of us

silently removed our laundry once a week and returned it folded and pressed the next day. She just as silently served us our meals in the breakfast room overlooking the fish pond. We always said thank you. She said nothing.

Her husband, skimming algae off the surface of the pond, occasionally glanced through the window at us, nodding his head ever so slightly.

"Okay," I said.

"Sometimes I think this place looks more like an abortionist's clinic behind the Iron Curtain than an autopsy parlor."

"What?"

"Nothing. Let's make some popcorn and see what's on the television."

"When can we go home?"

"I thought you liked it here. I thought this was an adventure."

"I just wondered. When?"

"Soon enough."

She turned out the lights and we ascended to the sitting room in the guest wing. *The Million Dollar Movie* was showing *While the City Sleeps*. We settled in to watch.

I touched the place on my chest where the head, unrecognizable, human, had touched me.

wartime

THE YEAR WAS 1974. I was walking on a dusty road above Cherbourg, wasteland on each side, on my way to the D-Day museum. There's not much to do in Cherbourg. Last night I saw *The Poseidon Adventure* dubbed in French.

A man is following me in a *deux-chevaux*. About ten yards behind me. As I go faster, so does he, but he maintains a distance, the pursuit. I can hear Cat Stevens on the radio. I worry that this is a wasteland. I hope he's only playing.

He persists, coming closer, and I turn and we make eye contact. He says something I don't get.

"Fool!" I yell at him, needing to say something, not wanting to set him off with something stronger.

"The French are so stunted," a friend of mine is fond of saying, ever since her lover went off with one of them.

Would that it were only the French. I remember the train from San Sebastian to Madrid, a man with a chicken in one hand, the other running itself under my skirt as I passed through the corridor. I turned; his wife, standing beside him. Both with gold teeth and smiles. I am well traveled.

The Frenchman suddenly blasts his horn a few times, U-turns, sending dust spiraling into me. Then gone. Just like that.

"Thank God," I say out loud.

Soon enough I reach the museum. I can see the cloud raised by the *deux-chevaux* at the foot of the hill.

No other company except the odd salamander.

The museum is divided into two parts. On the top floor, D-Day; downstairs, the Deportations. I am the only visitor. The curator, an older man with rosy cheeks, takes me by the hand. He leads me through the hodgepodge of the surroundings. The D-Day exhibits seem to consist of mementos scrounged from lost knapsacks. Canteens. C-rations. Snapshots. A flotilla made of children's boats sits on a blue-paper-covered table in the center of one room. Another table is covered with sand leading to precipices made of papier-mâché. I could be in someone's finished basement.

My father set up a Lionel train on a sheet of plywood he painted green. I was not allowed to touch but I was allowed to watch and to drop the smoke pellets into the locomotive's smokestack, one by one.

The curator leads me downstairs to the Deportations. The departed are memorialized by a gaunt statue, some newsprint and some photographs, and a list of names with numbers next to them, typed on an ancient machine, with much x-ing out.

The curator asks me if I am a Jew. When I say no, he

beckons me back upstairs. He asks me if I am American. When I say yes, his eyes light, and he speaks of the *gloire* of June 6, 1944.

But I turn back down the stairs, trace my hand over the list of names.

My mind starts to wander. I am recalling my senior year in college, when I worked as a receptionist in a tax preparer's office on Victory Boulevard and became acquainted with a Jew who had left both of his legs behind on Omaha Beach.

Almost everyone smoked in that office. Almost everyone smoked back then.

Jack Costello, the head accountant, took his place on a barstool next door to the office. It was the beginning of his daily routine. Eight A.M. and the owner was sweeping out the trash of the night before. Butts skated across the sidewalk in front of the broom, taking the slope of the concrete and tumbling into the gutter.

Jack sat with a shot of Scotch in front of him, the sun raking the plate glass window and his brain, gilding the liquid in the shot glass, showing up the infinity of rings within rings on the surface of the bar.

Jack was the first person I knew who treated alcohol like insulin, dosing himself steadily through the day, maintaining equilibrium enough to add column after column of figures, as his long fingers flew across the adding machine. As his left hand worked the keys of the machine, his right hand held a Pall Mall, and the blue smoke of unfiltered Turkish tobacco haloed his desk.

To look at him you never would have suspected he was a drunk.

He was, for one, impeccably turned out. Shined. Ironed. Brilliantined. Always in a three-piece suit, even when the City was suffering a wave of spring humidity and heat. Always decorated with a gold watch fob. Always with exactly one inch of gold-linked cuff showing.

If he liked you, he'd tell you all about the war and what a bastard Patton had been. And crazy besides. "The deranged son of a bitch believed in reincarnation. Thought he was Alexander the Great.

"And that was no accident," he said, referring to Patton's death. "His men did him in."

Jack claimed to have proof.

"The only proof Jack has is eighty proof," Fred Silvers said.

Fred was Jack's opposite. For one thing he never touched a drop.

"They put the son of a bitch in traction, with fishhooks through his cheeks."

For Fred the war seemed a lifetime ago. For Jack it was yesterday.

Fred couldn't remember which leg it was that had a scar from belly-whopping down Benziger Avenue, ending up under a milk truck, where a piece of the truck's exhaust tore through his pants and into his kneecap.

Fred wasn't an accountant. He leased space in the office during tax season and tried to get people to invest their refunds with Dreyfus. For the future, he told them. For security. Some of them barely glanced at the brochure he handed them, the lion emerging from the subway. Others gave him their attention, thought of security, but they were paying for what had passed, never mind what was to come.

Fred's interest in the future was newborn; he wanted to spread it around.

According to the way Jack told it, Fred had spent twenty-odd years in the back bedroom of a house in Levittown, his prosthetic legs propped against a chest of drawers. The legs changed over time, becoming lighter, more flexible. "Lifelike," Jack said, "if you weren't alive."

Fred's wife and their family doctor kept up with the latest models. Fred's wife changed the socks and shoes regularly. She kept the legs within his line of vision from the bed, where he was propped on pillows. She wanted to make the legs irresistible, so he would ask to strap them on, make her call the doctor to fulfill his desire to walk.

Her tender washing of the legs, oiling the knee and ankle joints, slipping the feet into argyle socks in winter, white cotton in summer, was ritual for her. "Like Mary Magdalene at the Last Supper," Jack said, speaking from his Catholic-addled brain.

When she put black executive hose and Thom McAn oxfords on the feet, Fred took her dancing. When she put on white tennis shoes, they strolled the beach, the boardwalk, rode the ferris wheel.

"It was so goddamned sad," Jack said. "She went into

debt for those legs. The VA would only cover the cheapest models, especially for a guy who refused to use them. Forget that. She needed them."

Fred's life might have ended there, had the Veterans of Foreign Wars not intervened, in the person of Jack.

"I just showed up one morning to talk to Fred," Jack said. "It was part of the program at the post.

"I told him he was wasting away."

"Why should you care?" Fred asked.

"There's a whole new world out there."

"So?"

"So why don't you go take a look?"

"This suits me fine."

"Television will rot your brain." *As the World Turns* droned in a corner by the legs.

"Maybe."

"Besides, soap operas are for housewives."

"It's only noise."

"I was there, too, you know."

"I figured."

"You want to know where?"

"No, thanks."

Jack admitted he needed to regroup.

"Excuse me a second."

"It's down the hall."

Sitting on the throne, Jack took a long draw from his flask, leaned back, and closed his eyes. "It came to me right there," he told me.

"Look, I'll make a deal with you."

"And what might that be?"

"Think of your wife."

"I do. All the time. It's really none of your business. Not that any of this is."

"We haven't forgotten you."

"You can't forget someone you've never known."

"I disagree. Look, if you give it a try, I'll take you to the track."

"What?"

"You'll love it."

"You must be nuts."

"There's nothing like it. We'll start small. Maybe Monmouth Park. Then the Big A. Aqueduct. How about it?"

And that brainstorm, Jack promised, was how he got Fred into the legs. "He was ready, that's all. I just provided the incentive."

Wherever the truth lies, Fred allowed Jack his story.

One Saturday afternoon in March 1969 is imprinted on my memory.

The door opens and a man staggers into the office.

There's a lull today, so Jack has his bottle of Johnnie Walker Black in full view. Fred has stopped by with lunch, which Jack barely touches.

"You can't live on whiskey alone, you know."

"I can try."

"You want to end up . . ."

Their conversation stops as each realizes the man standing just inside the door is wearing camouflage and his hands are trembling violently.

Jack looks him over.

"We don't keep any cash here."

The man only stares.

Fred pours some Scotch into a paper cup and offers the straggler a drink.

The man shakes out his hands three times, quick awkward motions, stopping the tremors long enough to take the cup from Fred.

"Thanks," he whispers. "Mind if I sit down?"

"Please." Fred balances himself on his legs and pulls out a chair for the man.

"How can I help you?"

"I came to get my taxes together. I have a letter from the IRS somewhere."

"Sixty-eight?"

"Since sixty-six I think."

"Well, let's get you started." Fred is speaking softly, taking on my usual job, filling out the top parts of the tax forms.

"Name?"

"James Franklin."

"Address?"

"You can reach me at the VA. I don't have the address on me."

"That's okay. I'll fill it in."

"Thanks."

"Occupation? Army?"

"Surgeon."

That gets everyone's attention. A silver caduceus that none of us noticed before is pinned to his fatigues.

"Something wrong?"

"Nothing," Jack speaks up.

"Back for good?" Fred asks.

"I think so. Not sure."

"Working at the VA?"

"Taking the cure."

"Tell him about the time Eisenhower stopped by your bed, Fred." Jack's intake appears to be out of whack.

"Don't mind him."

"I'll try."

"Tell him, Fred. If you don't I will."

"You know what, Jack? That never happened. It's just a war story."

"Don't kid a kidder, Fred."

I might as well be invisible. In fact I wish I was. A girl, one who marched against the war and probably will again, I feel ashamed, out of place.

"Hey, honey?" Jack startles me.

"Yes?"

"Here's twenty bucks. Go get me a fifth, will you? And keep the change."

"Come on, Jack. Enough is enough."

"Johnnie Walker got his gun, Fred. It's not just for me. It's for the doctor here. Don't forget, honey. Johnnie Walker Black, that's important. We don't want to insult the doctor."

Dr. Franklin makes no sign he's heard anything.

"I served under Patton." Jack has seized the floor. "The worst son of a bitch you ever want to see. Every son of a bitch has to come and bow down to that son of a bitch."

"Dr. Franklin?" Fred asks.

"Yes?"

"Did you really come here to get your taxes done?"

"It's almost time, isn't it?"

"Okay, then. Did you bring your documents?"

"Documents?"

"Lots been happening here since sixty-six," Jack says to no one.

"I guess I'd better come back."

"Do you have a way to get to the hospital?"

"I'll be fine."

"How'd you get here in the first place?"

"Cab."

"Let me call one for you."

"It's okay. Maybe I'll walk."

"Promise to come back."

"Right."

"No way in hell he took a cab. Who'd pick him up?" Jack says.

Dr. Franklin shoots him a look but says nothing. He gets up and leaves.

I'm still standing there with Jack's twenty in my hand.

"Well, honey, what are you waiting for?" There's a panic beneath the edge in his voice.

"I'll take that." Fred slips the bill from my hand and lays it on Jack's desk.

"You go home now. Make the rest of the day a holiday."

"Thanks, Mr. Silvers," I say, not exactly sure what he means, eager to be gone.

I turn and walk toward the door.

"Just imagine, Fred. A colored surgeon in the army. That wouldn't have happened in our day."

"No. It wouldn't," is Fred's reply.

I leave them through the glass door with the gold lettering.

My back is turned to the curator. I am looking out the window down at the Channel, and the beach, thinking about the decomposing of bones.

"La Manche," the curator says.

"Yes. I know."

He has a document in his hand. The folds of years threaten its integrity. It has a seal at one corner. He's holding it up against the window in the afternoon light. I can make out a watermark, a brown stain. The head of a helmeted female.

He points to a name. Points to himself. He folds the document along the same lines, tucks it into his breast pocket.

I thank the curator and leave the museum.

Outside the sun is high, pounding the dust on the hillside. I walk slowly toward the town. I feel like I've been away. Like leaving the dark of a Saturday matinee. The movie inside of me, not wanting to let it go.

art history

I

I PICK UP THE *New York Times* sometime in 1992 and find your name. My heart catches. We are twenty years from a summer filled with each other, and now I hear you laugh, and I sound foolishly romantic, now death is around us.

The first winnowing, a doctor said, cold. And if she is right, who will be left standing? This feels like a rout.

Riding uptown in a cab one spring evening in 1990 — it's important to get the years right; so much is happening, so fast — passing a bar called Billy's Topless, Angela musing, "I wonder if his mother knows?"

Arturo laughing.

Me between the two of them. She and I get out in the thirties, Arturo heads farther uptown. He's convinced the hotel's haunted by the ghost of Veronica Lake.

Two years later both he and Angela are dead.

"I'll call you when I'm in London."

His huge eyes. "We need a party."
But talk of that is for another time.

That summer you were subletting the apartment of an art historian in a brownstone just off Park, verging Spanish Harlem. Almost the top of the City, where the streets begin to broaden, becoming lighter, darker.

The art historian sent you a postcard from the Bomarzo, showing a picnic table between the legs of a gigantic stucco, stone, or terra cotta female. Her message was all business, then, underlined, "My favorite place to dine when in Italy." You showed it to me without a word.

The color in my cheeks rose higher and higher.

You were smiling. "Just once?" you asked.

I turned away, to the windows at the front of the apartment, overlooking the street, a playground, and some tenement walls plastered with Colt 45 and Newport ads in Spanish, and one wall that stood apart. On it shreds of a couple dressed in evening clothes framed a portrait of Bessie Smith. Someone had cast the Empress across brick, across ancient lettering advertising Madam's Rosewater, worn into "adam's Rose," elixir disappearing into her ermine wrap.

The light of the summer evening set the street to glowing, bathing the girls and boys in the playground, the men leaning against the anchor fence, the brown bags housing Ripple or Night Train or Thunderbird. Bessie Smith watching over them all. For a minute everything was golden, and then the evening shadows crept in.

"There's nothing like summer in New York," I said.

I turned around and kissed you goodbye.

"Why don't you stay?"

I was living downtown, in the Village, housesitting the townhouse of a former boss, whose copper-topped cocktail table I kept polished, whose mail I collected, and whose very gray portrait hung over the mantelpiece. She was perched on the edge of a chair, leaning forward, out of the plane of the picture, almost to launch herself into the room.

Her eyes were the same color as the suit she was posed in, close to charcoal, oddly missing the pinpoints of white, the light captive in the eye.

The painting was signed by her husband.

"Bill so much wanted a son," she told me as she showed me around the house, "and look what he got." We had ended up on the top floor of the slender building, in her son's room, painted black, with a purple ceiling, without furniture. "Absence," she said.

About a year before she had taken me to lunch at the Algonquin for my birthday. Because, she explained, they had the driest martinis in a five-block radius. I'd revealed to her that I'd never had a martini, and she said, "My God, you can't call yourself an American and not have had a martini."

She meant well and went ahead and ordered for me.

After she had drunk about three of them, she told me about her boy, actually a man, who set fire to the brooms at the Montessori where he worked as an aide. She talked about his need to fall from higher and higher places. She thought he was trying to fly, she said. "To leave himself behind and rise from the ashes.

"But it was no good."

After years of high places, and the places beneath, he fell from a window in Macy's, where he worked as a stockboy.

"One of those rainy New York nights," she said, "in November."

All of a sudden I thought of the Thanksgiving Day Parade and in my mind's eye caught a boy entangled in the guy wires of a balloon. Popeye's tattooed forearm floated by. I wanted to smile. It must have been the gin.

"I had to identify him. The morgue people didn't know what to do with me. They just stared, as if to ask, what kind of a woman has a son like that?"

I tried to engage her eyes but she was staring into her glass, into the bluish tinge of good gin.

"I didn't actually see what the fall had done. They had covered his face. I identified him from the nametag on his smock. But they told me."

I did not know what to say to her, except, "I'm sorry." It was one of those moments when I felt ignorant of some secret female gesture, something traditional I had never learned.

"Thank you," she said, "but I've only myself to blame."

For what? I wondered. Not breast-feeding him? Being a "career-woman"? Not wanting a child in the first place?

"Why should you blame yourself?" I asked, using the same tone I had learned to use with my father when he drank too much and became maudlin. I hated the sound of it, matching the unrealness of the drunken voice note for note.

"I should never have listened to them."

"Who?"

"The doctors. My husband. You have no idea how difficult artists can be. The last thing he wanted . . ."

"Oh," I said, unable to ask what.

"It was the fifties." She paused. Specters crowded in. "I like Ike." Betty Furness opening a sparkling white Westinghouse. *I've Got a Secret.*

"I didn't have a hell of a lot of options. Punishment and reward. That was the prescription. Please don't tell anyone about this."

"Of course not."

I wasn't sure what I'd heard.

I went back to my office, closed the door, and fell asleep.

We were standing in his room, at the top of the slender house, the door open to the fire escape, the perfect perch for a boy who wanted to fly.

In the purple ceiling and black walls were thumbtack marks, and I wondered what he had pinned there and what they would tell me if I knew.

She broke the silence in the room.

"There's one other thing about housesitting this summer. I probably should have mentioned this to you before."

"What is it?"

"If my son calls here you are under no circumstances to tell him where we are." She was cold sober, and her voice was unwavering although gathering speed. "And, if he asks to come here, you are to tell him *no,* in no uncertain terms. If he persists, or tries to get in, first call the precinct — they know all about the situation — then call us."

It had started to rain, a summer shower, sounding on the roof right over us, pelting the railing of the fire escape. The hot scent of summer mixing with rain came into the room, and she went on about the dead-alive boy.

I was, as they say in old novels, nonplussed.

"Damn, Bill and I better get going. He hates to drive in bad weather. The number in Wellfleet is by the phone in the kitchen. This is the first time in years Bill and I have had a place without room for Billy. There's no place for him with us anymore, there just isn't. Here, there, anywhere. You do understand, don't you?"

Hardly. But I nodded anyway, and when I found my voice I assured her, "Yes." I knew enough not to ask.

"Oh, and I'll leave a photo of him by the phone. It's a bit out of date, but it's the only one left. For God's sake don't fall for his poor soul routine."

"I won't," I said, and felt horrible.

As soon as they drove off I went into the kitchen. On a bulletin board next to the wall phone, between a postcard of a lighthouse and the takeout menu from the Good Woman of Szechuan, was the photograph of a boy. Dark, as if it had been taken at night with a flash. Crewcut, striped polo shirt, two-wheeler, vintage 1955 or so.

The landscape around the boy was nondescript. It could have been anywhere a boy like him might have been.

Central Park, maybe. Just some bushes and trees. In the darkness it was hard to tell much more. No suggestion of water, no shadow of a city skyline.

When I showed it to you, you thought he might be standing on the grounds of the place in *I Never Promised You a Rose Garden* or some other upper-class madhouse. Like Cascades in *Now Voyager*. Ice cream, tennis, Claude Rains.

"Where rich people send their kids," you said.

"Then why did she say . . . ?"

"She'd had a lot to drink. Maybe she has a drunken version and a sober version. Maybe she wishes he would."

"Jump?"

"Umhmm."

"Or maybe he's been standing by these bushes for twenty years."

I had no idea what I would do should he try to get in touch. I put the photograph away, in a drawer with playing cards and flashlight batteries.

I took the portrait from over the mantelpiece and hid it in a closet.

It was no use. Their shadows overwhelmed the place. I began spending more and more time uptown, returning to West 11th only to erase the tarnish from the copper-topped cocktail table and collect the mail.

One day there was a bill from someplace in the Berkshires, stamped *dated material, please respond* and the mystery seemed to be solved.

No matter.

✳   ✳   ✳

I slept with you in the art historian's bed, under a print of Michelangelo's *Night*. We slept like children at first.

But soon I woke to find my hand in the small of your back, linger there, becoming aware of your skin and mine. The evenness of your breath. The only sound in a room in a city with the windows open.

"What are you afraid of?" you asked me in the dawn.

"I want your mouth on me."

"Oh, that." You laughed in half-sleep.

Drawing me closer.

The art historian sent a postcard from a bar called Elle Est Lui. "I hope you've met my neighbors by now." Then: *"Toujours gai!"* signed Mehitabel.

Downstairs, in the garden apartment, were two painters, Judith and Alberto. She from Grand Island, Nebraska. He from a hilltown near Siena.

The art historian had not mentioned that Judith was dying.

As Alberto cooked, Judith talked almost nonstop, as if silence was a passage into the dark.

At first she entertained us with art world gossip. "Louise? Forget her. She just calls the foundry now. Doesn't even bother to stop by."

One of us mentioned the name of another woman artist, exploding into posters, calendars, notecards, threatening even Warhol with her promiscuity.

Judith smiled. "What's next?" she asked. "Sheets and pillowcases? A shower curtain with one of her wretched cow skulls?

"And she's never been sick a day in her life. Imagine. Just imagine."

As Judith spoke, the colored lights around the fountain in the back garden flickered. The water sprayed through the lights from the wide-open mouth of a dolphin, creating tiny, constantly changing patterns. The relentless exchange of form and color, light and water, helped take her mind off the pain, which the painkillers did less and less to mask.

We began to stop by there almost every evening.

"Here," she said suddenly, "this really belongs to you. I want you to have it."

She handed me a copy of *Wide Sargasso Sea*.

I looked at the jacket. A sad-looking young woman stood in the middle of an explosion of tropical lushness. She held a red hibiscus blossom. "Why?" I asked Judith. I didn't know the book at all.

"Because it's about your part of the world," she said. "How amazing to come from a place like that."

I only nodded, not having the heart to tell her what I actually thought of paradise. On the back of the book jacket was a familiar sight, the great house about to be swallowed by the green.

"Alberto and I were there once."

"Really? When?"

"A long time ago. Kingston was one of our ports of call on a voyage way back when. We took a freighter. We were only allowed to spend one afternoon ashore. When we got back the decks were piled high with bananas. And we were off, doing the bidding of United Fruit. I remember the mountains as this green approaching blue and the sea, my God . . . in the harbor dolphins skated by us. I was sitting on a pile of bananas, sketching like crazy. What must it have been like being a girl there?"

I always become wary when someone not of my ilk speaks of Jamaica, especially if I like the person. I wait for smiling or sullen natives, simple or crafty marketwomen, paradise lost on its inhabitants.

"It *is* a beautiful place," I said.

"I'm only sorry we weren't there long enough to get a real sense of it. We did see the boys diving for coins alongside the cruise ships. That was distressing."

I remembered those boys. There, as if they should be. Like the coconut palms, Her Majesty's sailors on leave, the maze at Hope Gardens, the viciousness of peacocks. Nothing was said in that part of the world when I was a girl. A truckful of marketwomen falling into a ravine. Screams into a Saturday night, then silence. I remember the headlights shining from below. People spoke of how the roadway was haunted, nothing else.

I was about to let her into a sliver of my girlhood, then I realized she had dozed off.

Judith didn't want any of her old friends or rivals "to see me like this," or so she said. Maybe she was afraid to ask them. I wondered if the remark about Louise not bothering to stop by referred to the foundry after all.

She said she was content with our company. "My new

friends, my girls. You know, I don't believe anyone dies of cancer. Not as long as you have company."

"You're probably right," you said.

"Yes," Judith said. "You have to be alone to die."

My mother had been. Maybe Judith was right.

I allowed myself the chance to look at you, your amber eyes rapt with her blue ones. I watched you take her hand, your fingers cradling hers, resting on the thing that covered her. She sighed. She gripped you tightly.

We sat there until the terror passed. For now.

"We should probably be going," I whispered, and you nodded, and that afternoon under the print of *Night* I made love to you, lifting and parting, lifting and parting, drinking you to my heart's content.

The next day we met for lunch in midtown and afterwards strolled through the Morgan Library. A guard showed us the murals in the ceiling over the old man's desk. Angelic or pagan forms gaped down, colors fading into wormed wood but for bright gilt around the borders. "From Lucca, Italy," the guard said, as if it were his ceiling, "I can tell you anything you want to know."

Judith sat across from her water and lights as Alberto cooked us chanterelles he'd gathered behind the reservoir in Central Park.

"Alberto goes mushroom gathering every day the day after it rains," she said.

The City had been washed clean the day before, that kind of hot rain that falls in August.

"Isn't this marvelous?" she asked us, holding up a tumbler. "They gave it to Alberto at a gas station."

G I A N T S was stenciled on the side of the glass in dark blue along with a football helmet.

"Alberto goes mushroom gathering and he also digs potatoes and onions. Guess where."

We both looked blank.

"Give up?"

"On one of those truck farms on Long Island," I guessed.

"Nope." She couldn't wait to tell us. "On the grounds of the Cloisters," she paused. "Honest."

"I kid you not," Alberto attested.

"Someone's kitchen garden from a long time ago. When the place was rural, before they put that pile of stones there. Imagine. Who were they? Whatever remains concealed in the middle of some bushes. The sweetest onions you've ever tasted. And the potatoes! My God. A kind from before all the crap they put into the ground. Some gnarled, misshapen, dented where they grew against rock. Nothing perfect."

"How did you find them?" I asked Alberto.

"I smelled the onions one afternoon. Very strong. I followed my nose to them. In Italian, *cipollini*."

"And garlic," Judith said, "and thyme and sage. Lavender. Don't you love the City? I find it very moving. Chamomile coming up through cobblestones."

"All through the City you find things like this," Alberto said.

"Anyplace people have lived a long time," Judith said. "There are vineyards in the depths of Staten Island."

It was a beautiful vision. The City as garden. The traces of others.

"Please come to dinner on Sunday," Judith invited us.

"Prego," Alberto said.

"Alberto has promised to trap a rabbit in Westchester — not as crazy as it sounds — and roast it on a spit in the fireplace for us. We'll put on the air conditioning full blast and pretend we're in the middle of a Russian winter instead of a waning New York summer. We must each choose someone to be. Someone who doesn't have cancer, that is."

"How about TB?" you asked, and Judith smiled.

"Yes, poor wretches, they all coughed, didn't they? All through those interminable novels — that or epilepsy, the Idiot and all that. No, we must be healthy Russians. No bloody handkerchiefs. Picture Catherine the Great, robust as hell I have no doubt."

"Can we bring anything?" I asked.

"Just yourselves. You may choose to be lovers."

She smiled up at us from her place on the couch.

"It's the drugs talking; you must excuse her," Alberto said.

"It is not, my darling; not at all."

You bent over her and kissed her, we said good night and turned to go upstairs.

"Just steer clear of Anna and Vronsky. Talk about the wrong side of the tracks." She laughed.

*　　　*　　　*

I stood at the bedroom window for a long time, looking out over Judith's fountain, the lights playing through the water, the water flowing from the dolphin. As long as there was light and motion I felt safe for her.

And then Alberto turned out the lights, shut off the flow of water, and I knew Judith had fallen asleep. That's how it would be. I hoped as much.

"Were you surprised?" You had come up behind me, your arm was around my middle.

"A little. Is it that obvious?"

"I do think she cares about us, you know."

"I just don't like having my mind read, that's all."

"Don't read disapproval into what she said, unless it's your own."

Boom! There it was, and I couldn't say anything.

You were looking into the darkness as the night breezes swung into the art historian's bedroom, lifting the corners of *Night*. The traffic noises, the breaking of glass across the way seemed to back off, and instead we heard Bessie Smith, her fine sounds, her blues.

The night with its half-asleep sounds, then the suddenness of the human voice raised in caress.

Sunday, as promised, a rabbit turned slowly on the spit, its fur wrapping to one side, folded in anticipation of another use.

Alberto wasted nothing.

He was at the sink blending a wild berry mixture into some yogurt.

Judith was all dressed up. Not as a Russian; that scheme

had been forgotten, or discarded. She was dressed as if for a gallery opening, all in black with a bright scarf wrapped around her burned head.

Around her, facing her on the tile of the kitchen floor, was her life's work.

One canvas was yellow. A bright chrome yellow. In the middle the painting seemed to tear and an underlayer of paint was revealed. Apparition of black beneath yellow. Dark behind light.

II

Judith died that September. In the middle of an Indian summer heatwave when there was a power failure and the lights around the City went out.

Stars were visible. The moon hung over the men in the playground.

The art historian returned from her travels with a woman she'd found at the Sound and Light show at the Colosseum in Rome.

My former boss sent a postcard of Highland Light and asked if I'd guard the townhouse one more month. "Bill and I have found each other again," she wrote, "who knows where this might lead?" P.S.: "We're thinking of adopting."

I ignored her request and called the precinct to tell them I had been called away and left the keys to the house with Captain January or whatever his name was.

part three

rubicon

THE RUBICON SPORTED but one neon sign in the window, advertising a locally brewed beer that no one within memory had ever ordered. Underneath the sign, in the right-hand corner of the glass, was a printed notice, WE RESERVE THE RIGHT TO TURN ANYONE AWAY.

The name of the bar was painted over the front door, the letters forming an arc above the entry.

This was the quiet end of the island, away from the skyline, the Statue of Liberty, the Quarantine Station at Ellis Island. This end of the island imagined another history. The Rubicon sat on a stretch of dead-end road between what was said to have been an Indian burial ground and the ferryboat to Perth Amboy. The burial ground was the terrain of high-school students, who tracked rats among the grassy mounds and necked in fin-tailed cars.

Some of the regulars at the bar came from the New Jersey side, crossing the Kill after work, catching the last boat back. Sailing, after hours, a passenger could make out beacons, pilot lights crowning the refinery drums like St.

Elmo's fire, like the Lady carrying her torch. Beacons light-
ing ordinary houses, laundry pinned to the line in all
seasons, against Esso, Shell, Sinclair encircling a bronto-
saurus.

The building that housed the bar was long and low,
somewhere between wartime Quonset hut and postwar
Levittown; tidy, nondescript. It stood solitary on its
stretch of road, the nearest neighbor the Conference
House where George Washington signed some papers.
That was a half-mile away, at night lit by the occasional
pass of a watchman's flashlight, by day the province of
schoolchildren led by their teachers and a couple of parent
(always mothers) volunteers.

If anyone entering the Rubicon expected a likeness of
Julius Caesar, a map of Gaul, assuming the name came
from someone's passion for ancient history — like the ele-
gantly suited Latin teacher who stopped in now and then
for Scotch, neat, who'd been attracted by the name in
the first place — they soon realized their error. The Latin
teacher glanced about the room, whispered to herself, "All
hope abandon, ye who enter here," relieved no one heard;
no one seemed to pay her any mind as she slid onto a barstool and ordered.

An eight-by-ten glossy taped to the wall over the cash
register, autographed "Straight from the Heart," informed
everyone that the name of the bar derived from its owners
— Ruby, Billie, and Connie — onetime girl singers with a
big band.

The only Latin these girls knew was Xavier Cugat.

In the photograph the girls wore matching evening gowns as they had on the bandstand, perched on gilt chairs (like the kind people rent for weddings), their hands gloved and folded in their laps, waiting for the bandleader to signal them with his baton and for them to "Take it away!" in three-part harmony.

The bandleader was Phil Gardner — he called the band the Philharmonics — and the circuit they traveled meant they would never collide with Artie Shaw or Tommy Dorsey, either on the charts or on the open road. Their bus, a pink curtain draped in front of the last couple of rows, flimsy privacy, took them through small towns as far west as Iowa, as far south as Kentucky, where they played in lodge halls and at county fairs.

"Those county fairs were something else," Connie said, tending bar one night. "The stories I could tell you. Not someone's pickles and preserves and flower arrangements. No. I learned about hookers at a county fair in Indiana. Honest. They kept the girls in a tent behind the midway. Who knows where they came from?"

"Made a change from pigs and sheep, I guess," Ruby said.

"Probably girls on the run," Connie said.

"Don't tell your father I brought you here," a woman was saying to a girl in a parochial uniform, the shield of St. Lucy over her breast pocket.

"Promise?" the woman asked.

The schoolgirl nodded.

"Please say it out loud, honey."

"I promise."

It was about four on a Thursday afternoon. The girl smiled briefly, as if to reassure, then turned her attention to her Coca-Cola, drawing it through a waxed paper straw, trying to trap the maraschino cherry on the end, then releasing it, drowning it once again.

"Okay," her mother leaned forward, "I'll be back in an hour or so, sweetie. Do you have something to occupy yourself while I'm gone?"

"Homework."

"Oh, well, here's a quarter for the jukebox in case you get bored."

The woman placed the coin next to the girl's school bag and got up to leave, turning toward the stairs at the right of the front door. Before she took her ascent she turned back to her daughter, mouthing "Promise?" which the girl, intent on her Coke, did not see.

The room upstairs was bathed in blue, the effect of a lampshade draped with a silk scarf. A dim winter light cast by a snow-promising sky barely grazed the window beside the bed. The bars of a space heater glowed red in one corner. A bunch of anemones, dead-of-winter extravagance, were opening in a glass jar on the windowsill, slowly, for the light was scarce.

Two women lay side by side on a chenille bedspread.

"Tell me."

"Not again. Hold me, please."

*   *   *

The jukebox sat at the far end of the bar, away from the front door, and featured selections from the heyday, such as it was, of Phil and his Philharmonics, with vocals by the Rubicon Sisters. "Collector's items," Billie liked to say. "Real museum pieces, honey. They couldn't have pressed more than a thousand, if that. We never saw a dime."

The schoolgirl had devised a game like Concentration to go with the display of song titles. But since the display never changed, at least it hadn't during the time her mother had been bringing her here, she soon committed it to heart and gave up her game. She wouldn't dream of playing the musical selections advertised — what was her mother thinking? — so the quarters accumulated in a jar in the top drawer of the girl's bureau, under a map of France on which she charted her future and imagined herself gone from that room.

Now, finished with her Coke, she wondered what to do next. Her mother's promise of an hour was never an hour. The girl stared at the hands of her wristwatch, trying to detect movement. She finally got up and walked over to the window, looking out into the street, noticed she hoped by no one. None of these women ever bothered her but she felt conspicuous, odd.

The only person sitting at the bar that Thursday afternoon was Patty, nursing a gin and tonic. A summer drink in the dead of winter. Close your eyes and you were at a backyard barbecue surrounded by regular Americans, some of whom you were related to. Ye gods. She shivered.

"Someone just walked over my grave," she said, addressing no one.

In the back of the room, to the back of the girl, a few couples were scattered at tables with parchment-shaded lamps on which red-coated hunters chased a fox. Smoked yellow light raked each tabletop. The walls around the tables were hung with memorabilia, handbills and posters, in the dark like the past, future.

The place was quiet but for the hum of the cooler.

The TV over the bar was tuned to *The Edge of Night* with the sound off. Patty preferred it that way. And since she was the only one at the bar it was her call.

Someone was on trial. The judge banged his gavel. Someone was pointing at the front row of spectators in the courtroom.

The girl turned from her view of the empty street and glanced up at the silent screen.

"You are my heart urchin."

"What's that?"

"A sea creature."

"I wish there was somewhere else we could go."

"Ever try to figure out what they're saying?" Patty spoke in the direction of the girl.

"Sometimes."

"It's fun, isn't it?"

"I guess."

A slope-backed Chevy takes a turn, moves down the street toward the building in late-afternoon winter light. The light makes the day colder. Makes some people long for the dinner hour, when they will be inside, safe, the driver thinks, TV tuned in, minute steak or fried chicken or spaghetti on a table set with a tablecloth. The radio in the car is tuned to the news but the driver is not paying any attention. The car slows, slides next to the curb, idles. The driver cracks the window, takes a deep breath of cold air. Everything is gray, upholstery, dashboard, sky, building, the afternoon. But for the car, which is black, and the end of her cigarette glows red.

"Hey, Patty?" Connie emerged from the back room, a case of Seagram's about to slip from her arms.

"Yeah?"

"Give me a hand, will you?"

"Sure."

Patty stood down from her barstool and went over to Connie. Between them the two women hefted the box onto the surface of the bar.

"Thanks, hon. Let me get you one on the house."

"No, I'd better not."

"Plans?"

"God, how I hate going out that door."

"Can I get you another Coke?" Connie had turned to the girl.

"No, thank you."

"There's cheese and crackers, if you're hungry. They're free."

"I'm not hungry."

"Okay. Well, if you change your mind, it's right here. Just help yourself."

"What a life," Patty said.

"It'll do," Connie responded.

"Why don't you let me get you a cup of coffee before you go?" Connie asked. "It's awful raw out there."

"Okay, thanks." Patty settled back on her barstool, not ready to leave, not just yet.

The Edge of Night had given way to *The Secret Storm.*

The driver of the Chevy is in danger of running down the battery. She turns the key in the ignition, the engine revs up and the car pulls away from the curb and continues slowly down the road.

Through the gray, snow starts to fall. Lightly. Lightly coating the branches of birches at the side of the road. The driver turns on the wipers, turns the car around, and makes her way to Hylan Boulevard. She turns left at the corner and heads down the boulevard toward the ferry to Perth Amboy. She passes Wolf's Pond Park and remembers a picnic some years back. She and some other high school seniors, cheerleaders all, entertained a group of boys from the Mount Loretto Children's Home. She remembered her boy very well. Olive-skinned with curly brown hair, he was about eight and she gave him a baseball glove. He said to her, "I'll have to ask Sister to put this away for me." From the boy the chain of memory takes her to one particular girl, who got pregnant and was expelled and disappeared from all their lives the fall of their senior year. The driver later met her in a supermarket but nothing was said.

The car stops at the edge of the Kill and she turns around and heads back to the bar, where she will sit for a while and wonder what is on the other side of the door.

"Waiting must be pretty boring," Patty says.

"It's okay."

Like most rituals — and Thursday afternoon has become ritual — boredom is one aspect.

Each Thursday afternoon her mother picks her up at school and says, "I have to make one stop on the way home. Okay, sweetie?"

And the girl says, "Okay."

And the ritual continues with the question her mother asks her in the bar, and her promise.

As long as this remains ritual, as long as whatever happens upstairs does not come downstairs, everything will be as it is and has been. Ritual contains.

So the waiting is okay.

apache tears

APACHE TEARS is a small community thirty miles east-northeast of downtown Los Angeles. Unlike most of the communities that impinge on the city, Apache Tears is discrete, the secret of a canyon as the desert begins, set out by a railwayman who longed for his hometown and worshipped the orderliness of a grid.

Apache Tears is the kind of place where, at the end of the twentieth century, milk is delivered to the front door, placed on porches in wooden boxes stamped in red APACHE TEARS DAIRY, contained in glass bottles with cardboard stoppers stamped in black HOMOGENIZED.

Not a silhouette of a missing child in sight. No "Have you seen me?" (And what would you do if you had?) next to a lost face. Rather the bottles are etched with a herd of Jersey cows standing on the deck of a clipper ship heading around the Horn in the nineteenth century. Brave cows, lashed to the mast in a gale.

Cream, eggs, orange juice, and butter are also available, and a milkman with the teeth of a puppy and a black plastic bow tie leaves a pad and pencil for the lady of the house to communicate her wishes.

He visits in the dark, ending his tour of Apache Tears just as the sun begins its rise. Few have seen him, but many lying between dreamtime and waking have heard the gentle rattle of milk bottles being exchanged. This lends them comfort and allows them another few moments of rest.

WELCOME TO APACHE TEARS, the sign says at the edge of town, IF YOU'RE QUIET, YOU'LL NEVER HAVE TO LEAVE. Some believe this motto had its origin when Alfred Hitchcock scouted the town as a location for *Shadow of a Doubt* only to settle on Santa Rosa up north. Others have their doubts.

The town of Apache Tears is entirely self-contained. Along with the dairy, there's the Apache Tears Agricultural Project, the Apache Tears *Clarion,* Apache Tears College, the Apache Tears Bach Society, the Apache Tears Medical Center, and what some consider the crown jewel, the Apache Tears Museum, presided over by the town raptor.

The Museum is at first glance unassuming, kept in a residence on one of the many tree-lined streets. Apparently just another Victorian, one of many on streets past clean, fronted by lawns so green, cut so close, they might have been painted (as Santa Barbarans were forced to do in the years of drought). Water tells the story of much of the West and Apache Tears owes its well-being to an underground river, diverted by means of dynamite and careful planning. This is the edge of the desert after all. Desert scrub, creosote mountains blacken the horizon. Joshua trees stark as a lynched hombre, rattlers that go straight for the nervous system, chasing the victim into unconsciousness.

None see past the danger of the desert into its tender nature. It blooms at its heart.

It surrounds them.

Small black stones mark the town's perimeter.

Perfectly folded newspapers lie each at the same angle on the flagstone walks, while lines of porch swings move gently in the clear morning air. Doors are opened, greetings exchanged, the day has begun.

The town raptor is a woman, a natural-born collector. She has been drawn to collecting since childhood. Of course many children collect, have collected. The usual things: baseball cards, seashells, rocks, bottle caps, dolls from around the world. The raptor stands apart from the usual. Her speciality since childhood has been the possessions of the dead.

And she's a natural.

There is very little gossip in Apache Tears so it's hard to tell where the raptor got her enthusiasm for death, and back issues of the *Clarion* shed no light.

In the depths of her walk-in closets upstairs is an extraordinary array. Clothes of every age, type, but also accouterments, medicaments, passports, cigarette lighters, diaries, tie clasps, canned goods, bridgework, handkerchiefs, watches, eyelash curlers, moisturizers, corkscrews, car keys, bracelets, lockets, stacks and stacks of ticket stubs, bowling shoes, golf balls, catgut rackets.

From the expanse of those closets to the public rooms on the first floor, the heart and soul of the museum, the raptor has proved herself the best at what she does. But who's to compare?

She dresses herself from the upstairs closets and descends to greet visitors at the front door. She is in a way the first exhibit, a taste of what is to come.

One day she may sport the leather jacket of a dead lover, lean on the shooting stick of a departed Jesuit, wear the eyeglasses of a cleaning woman stricken on the job, drape her neck with a locket containing the hair of an infant found in the trash behind the Apache Tears Motel (the *Clarion* reported an outbreak of measles), paint her nails with the savage choice of a long gone (but not forgotten) actress.

She will tell visitors to the museum about the dead she wears that day after a fashion. They expect from her the unexpected, the strange, never knowing who will greet them, interrupting their dailiness. This is prologue.

She will lead them into the public rooms and tell them again how she circumvented everyone, from local police to U.S. Customs, transporting bits and pieces from the burial places of Sumeria and Crete, the graves of Hittites and Etruscans, the inner chambers of Egyptians, and, closer to home, with only reservation cops between her find and her station wagon, the leavings of Hopi and Acoma, bones that sing.

From one wall, in what would be the dining room were this an ordinary place, the feathered burial robe of a Hawai'ian elder threatens flight. Illusion.

In her guide to the collection, the raptor goes into great detail about the process of acquisition. The guide covers everything from the beginning of the raptor's passion, excising childhood. The raptor, whose face is not reflected in the hall mirror, quicksilver worn away in a nun's cell, explains that her mentor was her first and only husband, a necrologist who led her by the hand from her freshman year at Apache Tears College into the days of the dead of the rest of the world.

She left him behind once she was expert, she says, and when she found him pissing into the embalmed mouth of a Javanese princess, which remains unsaid.

The artifacts are confused. Restless.

A Sumerian beanpot intended for the next world is lost in southern California on a shelf at the edge of the desert in a place with its back to the desert, encircled by small black stones.

```
     pots     shards     rattles     gourds     urns
words           pictograph
                          petroglyph           message
code            allusion          poetry    quip   devotion
     gods they know          gods who make love
                to them
                               who make fun
          of them
```

    outlines of the ghost-dance on a buckskin shirt
dance them into the sea
                  dance them off
when grasses are high
into the Great Silence.

on a beach thousands of miles away a female is tossed up
slashes across her breast   lines etched by iron
            trace of a braid   face
the sea was not responsible for this   for you
           some someone was   sweetheart
echoes collide in this silence
unheard by the raptor, who looks at these things, strokes
them, relies on their company, but cannot imagine their
awful noise.

Loneliness.
    Like the aboriginal child waking at twenty-five to no
memory. Is she not fortunate?
    Their properties may drift. Cut from their gods as they
are, their dreamtime. They may become corrupt. Then
what? What may be summoned?
    This place is not the toy shop after dark (Toyland, Toy-
land, wonderful girl-and-boy-land Follow the bouncing
ball!), after the Gepetto has gone home and the marionettes
and tin soldiers and porcelain ballerinas make merry.
    Things linger.
    In the back room under lock and key, in the chamber
where the raptor works, in what would be the butler's
pantry were this an ordinary place, something bobs in a

jar of spirits. The liquid turns blood-red as the sun drops.

Outside the town limits, in the desert proper, beyond the stone circle is a settlement known to outsiders as Cactusville.

Cactusville consists of a few motels, a gas station, a taquería, a convenience store that once had a million-dollar winner. Like the infant found in the Dumpster behind the Apache Tears Motel, a million-dollar winner seemed an anomaly in a dried-up place like Cactusville.

The motels are from the forties, fifties, miniature Mission revival, small adobe rooms facing a central courtyard. The residents of those rooms come from across the border, down Mexico way, and travel to the fields in school buses with portable toilets strapped to the back of the bus.

At the border, behind the streams leading from the *maquilladoras,* there is an outbreak of anencephalic children.

The lottery winner left behind a snapshot, which the convenience store manager displays over the lottery ticket dispenser. He has drawn a jagged outline around her, fixed false roses at each corner, and cut a crescent moon from cardboard that he has placed at her feet. A line of red glasses with white candles stands in front of her, on top of the lottery ticket dispenser, and *milagros* hang like earrings around this apparition of Nuestra Señora de la Lotéria.

Outside the convenience store, out back in the arroyo once coursing with water from underground, where wild grapevines coiled around telegraph poles, a Mojave rattler draws circles in the dust, knowing his protective coloring cannot save him.

a public woman

IN HER ROOM she saw what she thought was the apparition of a knight dressed in silver, with a plumed helmet. The plume appeared black in the black and white of midnight but could have been crimson or indigo. The figure did not vanish when she opened and shut her eyes and she reckoned — however much reckoning anyone can do in the dead of night, suddenly woken — he could not be inside her mind. He must be in her room.

Slowly the silver coat, glinting in the dark of the small bedroom, the one she kept for herself, marched toward her and she could make no difference.

Under its thrall she could make no sound.

No one would ever know her real name, her point of origin.

Among her effects were:

> 1 blue plaid silk dress
> 1 red moiré dress and cloak

1 gold hunting watch
1 silver cup, inscribed J. C. B.
1 silver brick, marked with the same initials
1 jet breastpin

A filigreed ivory cylinder carved with bearded monkeys and split pomegranates, extraordinary work, very fine. Inside the cylinder, like a curled prayer, was a piece of parchment coated with a sticky substance. At first glance, black characters dotted the parchment, underlining the apprehension that here was some sort of text. Silk ribbons hung from the top of the cylinder, which the coroner had untied from inside Jule's drawers. The whole gadget was the size of a fountain pen.

A mystery in the middle of a mystery until a closer look revealed the black characters were not a Chinese prayer for the dead (the thing had an oriental look to it, the investigator thought), or the last will and testament of a public woman, but trapped fleas. The investigator remarked that he had heard of such things (he couldn't call it an ornament despite the delicacy of its design) but he'd never seen one up close, much less handled one.

The flea-catcher made the two men, coroner and investigator, smile.

There was no escaping the ignominy of sudden violent death.

Next to the bed, next to her body, on a deal table she'd ordered all the way from England, was a framed tintype. The background of the picture appeared to be painted, like the backdrop on the stage of Piper's Opera House in

Virginia City. She'd gone there one afternoon for the phenomenon of Jenny Lind and noticed the scenes of the Comstock, the advertisements over the singer's head (Lafayette Beef & Veal & Pork; Star Restaurant; Davis Master Stationers; Imperial Hotel) and above them, dead center, a portrait of William Shakespeare.

The wealth of the Comstock drew all manner of unimaginable beings to it, like the Swedish Nightingale, like Jule's silver knight.

The background of the tintype had a garden urn mounted on a carved pillar beyond which was a tree with hundreds of small oval leaves. To one side of the two human figures in the foreground was a drawn-back curtain, apparently brocade, either real or *trompe l'oeil*, it was hard to say. The floor on which the two figures stood was covered by a carpet with rings and rings of roses.

The two human figures were another mystery. Neither was recognizable as Jule. One was a dark-skinned woman in a taffeta (or what looked like taffeta) dress, but not African, dark from somewhere else. And next to her stood a man in a morning coat and striped trousers, light-colored mustaches dripping at either side of his mouth. A pickax in his left hand, against which he rested.

The investigator studied the tintype, could draw no conclusions except the obvious: The man was a miner, the studio portrait perhaps to commemorate a strike.

The investigator laid the picture beside her other effects.

On a writing desk in a corner of the room was a page

facedown on the blotter. The investigator carefully turned it over.

> January 20, 1867
> Paid O'Hara $5 for squaw-washing.
> Burning sensation, outweighed by relief.
> Brandy. Then bed. No company.

> January 21, 1867
> Egg passed safely. No ill-effects of the washing.
> Fed a group of hand-carters who came to the door.
> Awful late for emigration I said.
> Said they'd had enough and were headed back.
> Don't know how they pitched up on this side of town,
> amongst all us female boarders.
> Didn't ask anything.
> Directed the women to the public baths.
> Men stayed behind to rearrange the goods on the carts.
> No children with them. I know enough not to say anything.
> Gave the men some Sazerac while the women were gone.

"Never heard of a whore keeping a diary," the investigator said.

From time to time the investigator visited the parlor houses overseen by madams, the lowdown hurdy-gurdy houses, the rows of cribs — called stockades — inhabited by girls on their own.

All women were hard to know, to be sure; whores, the "fair but frail," the most opaque of all. There was an apparent boldness to women who called themselves Big-Mouthed Annie (and not because of her volubility), the Big Bonanza, the German Muscle Woman, but who were they really; where had they come from? The streets of this and every other boomtown were filled with women from all parts, each covering her trail.

And when the mines began to fail, as they must, and the towns became skeletal, the women faded. Tokens for their services encrusted with the cryptobiotic desert, embossed with their monikers, Dianne the Queen, Skidoo Babe, Jew Ida.

Julia Bulette, known as Jule, was one of these.

Her name had not been given her; like the others, she'd taken it.

Her place of origin was said to be London, or New Orleans, or Istanbul. Or all three. Her closest friend was believed to be Glorious Holmes, neighbor and whore, with whom she took breakfast and lunch, to whom Jule read aloud (but the investigator would not suspect this). Glorious Holmes claimed to be a renegade Mormon, turning the life of a plural wife inside out, a price on her head by the busy little bees.

On the narrow shelf bordered by a slender brass rail at the top of the writing desk was a silver tray in which a *carte de visite* lay, inscribed *Jule,* in black italic script, printed by Davis Master Stationers, who'd advertised their services above the head of Jenny Lind.

Jule worked alone. Her only employee was someone known as the Chinaman who came to her house early each morning to build a fire. It was he who found her body, was questioned (although he spoke almost no English), and was released to the Chinese side of town where on his own he warned the Chinese whores of his discovery.

In the center of the bed the body lay, a counterpane covering her face. Underneath the covers was her slit throat, her blood collecting, draining into the mattress, running onto the carpet into the floor.

The trouble with the murder of a whore, the investigator said to the coroner, is that the number of suspects grows according to the popularity of the whore. And since whores don't keep very good records, well then.

"If a married woman is murdered, you have a number one suspect right there, who usually turns out to be the culprit. Same with a girl who's spoken for. But with whores, well, you know."

"Indeed I do," the coroner said.

They finally did arrest someone. An illiterate Frenchman with the name (given or taken) of Jean A. Villain who was caught peddling a blue silk dress with the initials J. C. B. embroidered inside the neckline. Glorious Holmes affirmed that the dress belonged to Jule, and Sam Rosener, the local dry goods merchant, testified he'd sold the cloth to Jule.

That was that.

Villain hanged for Jule's murder in front of a crowd of three thousand, including Mark Twain, a reporter for the *Territorial Enterprise,* who attended with his colleague William Wright (pen name Dan De Quille).

*   *   *

Some weeks before

To the Estate of Julia Bulette

1 Mahogany Coffin	$ 75.00
1 Plate & Engraving	10.00
1 Merino Shroud	20.00
1 Wreath of Flowers	3.00
1 Escort in Attendance with Hearse	25.00
	$133.00

Payable to J. W. Wilson

EVERY VARIETY OF FUNERAL EQUIPMENTS
EXHUMATION & SHIPPING A SPECIALITY

Her burial took place in a rage of a snowstorm.

We are left with the mystery of which the investigator and coroner were unaware, but neither could imagine the dream of a public woman, or the last thing she saw. Nor should we blame them.

The man in silver in her room whom she apprehended as a knight with a plumed helmet.

Glorious Holmes paid the funeral costs. "It's the least I can do," she said.

Eventually the street was razed. Under its ruins, washed up by winter rains, was a glass douche, patented 1857.